T0065216

ORPHANS

FRANK DEWEY STALEY

ORPHANS

iUniverse books may be ordered through booksellers or by contacting:

iUniverse
1663 Liberty Drive
Bloomington, IN 47403
www.iuniverse.com
844-349-9409

ISBN: 978-1-6632-2777-5 (sc)
ISBN: 978-1-6632-2778-2 (e)

Print information available on the last page.

iUniverse rev. date: 08/17/2021

Dedication

To Elizabeth, Alex, James, Frank and Scarlett who
keep me young and age me in equal portions.

1998

The night that her boss knocked on her hotel room door a few minutes before midnight just to make sure, for the second time that evening, that she didn't need a backrub was the night Isabel Storey decided to become a thief.

She had worked for Malcolm Crawley for almost two years and had grown to expect a certain amount of slimy and suggestive behavior as part of these business trips. What did break the trend of normal creepiness this night was that Crawley didn't get the hint. Probably more accurately, he got the hint loud and clear, but after a few drinks at dinner chose decisively to ignore it.

This was at a time when many men in the business world still recognized sexist behavior more as a perk than a pitfall. Crawley was a man of his time; at least that's how he would have rationalized his behavior if he gave any time at all to contemplation.

"Malcolm, it's late and I need to get some sleep. I still have some work to do before our meeting with the station tomorrow," said Isabel. "Thank you, but I'll see you in the morning at breakfast."

"OK, but it's your loss," he said. "We could have a hell of a time."

Five minutes later, when Isabel finally trusted that the propositions were ended for the day, she slipped into bed. Although tired from a long day of travel, of work and of fending off Crawley's only-slightly nuanced advances, she couldn't get to sleep. Never one to make a motion without fully fleshing out every conceivable outcome, she began to plot the course of action that would make her a woman with a big bank account.

Isabel's path led her to Crawley's orbit only a couple of years after graduating from college. She had been an extraordinary student through high school and was given a scholarship to Ohio University in Athens. Schools at the time were looking for well-rounded kids, and the fact that Isabel was not only bright, but had been the captain of the soccer team ensured her entry and the financial aid that went with it.

Her first job out of school was as a team leader for a consulting firm. She liked the travel that went with the position but loved the ability to fully immerse into so many different types of businesses. She quickly developed a reputation as a no-nonsense worker. She typically worked well into the evening getting up to speed on the workings of the operations she was tasked with analyzing. Her real strength was on display when it came time to implement the changes her analyses suggested. She was fair but firm; she listened, but the road map she had developed towards improved performance was not subject to alteration. She was, despite her youthful appearance and the fact that she was often the only woman in a male-dominated world, supremely professional and affective. After two years of out-performing everyone in her division, she was passed over for a promotion to be the Director of Field Ops. The explanation she received, that she needed a bit more seasoning, did not dissipate her disappointment.

Kalkan Communications had sought a business manager to help run the company's many operations. Kahlil Khan, the company's owner, had built up a relatively diverse empire from scratch. The son of desperately poor Afghan immigrants, Khan had put himself through college working at the school's radio station. A degree in marketing and the hands-on knowledge of running an audio board proved to be all he needed to begin the long march toward serious wealth. He was tight with a dollar, sought out undervalued properties and screwed every single person with whom he made a deal.

Isabel was selected with two other candidates to run the gauntlet of final interviews with Khan and Malcolm Crawley. In a break with normal business protocol, the type of which she would eventually come to see as Khan's standard operating procedure, all three candidates were invited to meet their interviewers simultaneously for lunch. The awkwardness was only surpassed by the lack of flavor in the food. Ginny's Diner was a cafeteria-style eatery in downtown Memphis that specialized in over-steamed vegetables, heavily salted slabs of ham and beef, and biscuits and breads of all kinds. Jello served with non-dairy whipped cream was a dessert option. Khan had invested in the place several years earlier. He liked the food and the prices. He was not a fan of the fact that Ginny served dozens of homeless men and women without charging them a nickel, but he came to grips with it. Charity was not a strong character trait he possessed.

Kahlil Khan was a small man who wore a light colored suit and patterned tie every day of his life. He drove a large Cadillac and lived in a mansion on the outskirts of Memphis. His fingernails were perfectly manicured, and his thinning hair was dyed an unnatural shade of red…a color only a child melting together an assortment of crayons could duplicate. He possessed the mannerisms and disposition of a Southern gentleman and had the yellow eyes of a pigeon. Despite being a millionaire many times over he never tipped.

Isabel stole the show. She answered with a firm deference and projected an ability to handle problems directly and without needing guidance. She had done her homework; she cited several of the operations in the Khan Empire by name and by location. In the end, Khan wanted to hire her for her for her business sense; Crawley, who had been unable to keep his eyes off Isabel's athletic and very shapely body, couldn't wait for their first road trip. The other two candidates, both men, had not had a chance in hell of joining this circus.

Isabel had joined the company at an exciting time. The growing empire of Kalkan in 1998 consisted of five television stations, a dozen radio properties, a golf course and several car dealerships. Khan also held ownership positions in businesses as diverse as the diner to a father and son trucking company.

When she asked Crawley why each wing of the company was its own entity, he shook his head.

"I know, it makes very little sense," he said. "The accounting alone is a nightmare. I've asked Mr. Khan a hundred times to pull everything in together into one operating model, one budget. But he won't do it."

"What's his concern?" asked Isabel.

They were sitting in Crawley's office. Isabel wore a gray suit with a green blouse. Her black heels looked expensive but were not. She rested a note pad on her lap and made notes with a yellow, number two pencil.

"This place has grown up organically, one little bush at a time," said Crawley. "Mr. K started with the station in Biloxi…that's actually where we were set up the first couple of years. Bought it with another guy and then moved him out. I think he's always been afraid that one property might pull the others down, so he's kept the structure kind of piecemealed. I mean, it's not how you or I would do it, but it's his bunch of bushes. And he's forgotten more about making money than we'll ever know."

Crawley's office was larger than a man of his physical stature should possess. He had professed to be a Navy fighter pilot in Vietnam, an instructor of hand-to-hand combat at the Academy in Annapolis and a self-made millionaire in his own right. Isabel considered only the last claim to be plausible. A picture of Crawley in full flight suit regalia standing comfortably next to his jet would have helped his cause. There was none.

She looked him over at intervals of note taking and tried to picture him in hand-to-hand anything. This was the most dubious of his claims; his wrists were the size of celery stalks, he possessed not one hint of muscle tone and the pigmentation of his rather translucent skin suggested, at best, hemophilia.

"So, how did you join the company, Malcolm?"

"I had just gotten out of the service and finished business school. My dad had done some work for Mr. K…

due diligence kind of stuff. I hired on as a radio station manager and worked my way up. Trust me, I brought a lot of money-making properties to the table. I've made this company a lot of money."

Isabel would learn to filter much of Crawley's braggadocio through a lens of questioning credibility, but some of this actually made sense. Crawley was not stupid. He owned several businesses on the side and Isabel learned quickly not to bother him with Kalkan stuff in the event he was immersed in his own dealings.

"By the way, that's a very nice suit you have on, Isabel."

"Thanks," she said in hopes that a brief answer would lead to a change of subject.

"You must work out," said Crawley. "You have a terrific body, girl."

Isabel looked at her note pad. Indignation percolated up from her throat but stopped just short of formulating words. She was still new at this time, and Crawley no doubt could have talked Mr. Khan into replacing her with a short conversation. She made a business decision and swallowed hard.

"Thanks, Malcolm. I go to the gym every night after work. I'm glad it's paying off."

"So, how do you like Memphis?" he asked. "Any boyfriends yet?"

"I like it here, but I'm kind of focused on my work for now. So, the company was actually in Biloxi for a while?"

"Yea. Don't worry, I'll take you down there for a tour of the station one of these days. They make great gumbo down there. You like spicy, Isabel?"

"Love it," she said as she stood to leave.

Although the laws of physics precluded it, Isabel was certain she could feel Crawley's intent gaze on her ass as she exited his office.

Those early days at Kalkan were not all bad for Isabel, but they all did prove to be consistently unconventional. She had very little contact with Mr. Khan; he stayed to himself in his large office on the top floor of the building. On the rare occasions she was granted an audience with him, she was dragged along by Crawley as a resource. She sensed early on that Malcolm expended more energy on his own business interests than on the company's, and that he worried about being asked a question the answer to which he could not provide. Crawley had been with Khan from the outset, but the old man's willingness to cut marginally-productive employees off at the knees was legendary. Isabel was along to provide supporting data and insightful analysis when Crawley stumbled.

On one such occasion several months into Isabel's tenure with Kalkan, Mr. Khan asked her to stay a moment after Crawley had left. She sensed massive nervousness from Crawley; his thin and poorly shaved neck reddened and perspired immediately. He took several seconds too long to gather his notes and shuffle to the door.

"Don't worry, Malcolm. It will just be for a moment," said Khan.

When Crawley had exited and closed the door behind him, Khan asked Isabel to sit. Isabel Storey had prided herself in an ability to predict the future; she was rarely surprised. At this moment, however, she had no clue.

"Isabel," said Khan, "I just wanted to tell you how happy

7

we are that you're with us. You are doing a great job, and I'm very pleased that you're with our company."

"Thank you, Mr. Khan. Trust me, I feel exactly the same way. I look forward to being an even greater contributor to Kalkan. I have some ideas about operations that I'll run up through Malcolm when I've fleshed them out."

Khan sat at his massive desk as a child sitting in the driver's seat of a parent's car. It all seemed too big for him. His suit was pastel blue. He wore a firmly-pressed white shirt and a paisley-print tie. Isabel would have been surprised to know that his socks, safely hidden under his massive desk, were bright yellow.

"There's something I want to ask you to do for me," said Khan.

"Name it, sir," said Isabel. Although the preamble to Khan's question could have been ominous, she sensed that the old man had not one hint of Crawley in him. Kal Khan was a gentleman; of that she was fairly certain.

"You've met Buster and Allie. What are your thoughts on them?"

This was a question loaded with the potential for danger, but no more so than with opportunity. Buster and Allie Khan were the thirty-something year-old children of Kal and Marissa Khan. They each occupied swank offices on the third floor of the building; they each drove Mercedes sedans; they each wore impeccably-tailored suits. Of interest, and what had been apparent to Isabel from the moment she met them, was that they each possessed not one ounce of understanding or ability to run a business.

"First," she said, "you need to know that they both have been very gracious in the way they've accepted me into the company. They have both been so forthcoming and supportive. You know, Mr. Khan, there are a lot of companies with family members involved where the family members don't make the kind of contributions to the bottom line that Buster and Allie do. You're very lucky that they are as committed as they are."

Khan knew a smooth line when he heard one, but he had a genuine soft spot for his kids. He nodded at Isabel's assessment. Buster and Ally remained oblivious to the minutia of running the empire. They both were, however, gifted at remaining silent and projecting the affectation of a furrowed brough.

"Isabel, I would like you to take Allie under your wing. I know she's a bit older than you, and that she's been with the company for much longer. But I see in you someone who has skills she does not possess. I want you to teach her how to run the business from a broader perspective. Expand her horizons a little."

Isabel recrossed her legs and flipped her light brown hair to one side.

"I'm honored, sir. I truly am. And I'll do exactly as you say. I'll be delighted to work closely with Ally."

She paused for effect.

"One question, though, Mr. Khan. How will I do this without insulting Ally? I'm not sure she'll be open to my becoming her mentor."

"I'll handle that," said Khan. "I'll tell her I want her to work closely with you so that she can help you along, that she can mentor you. She'll go with that, and it will give you all the opportunity you need to help her expand."

Business completed, Khan thanked Isabel and placed

his phone to his ear. He did not look up as she exited the office and gently closed his door.

Moments later, when she had settled behind the desk in her much smaller office on the third floor, Crawley darkened her door.

"What did the old man want?"

"He really just wanted to welcome me and tell me he was pleased with the work I was doing. Jesus, what a nice and thoughtful man."

Crawley suspected more but lacked the courage to dig further. Whatever Khan really wanted was the question, but to answer it would have involved a discussion in the office on the top floor. Malcolm Crawley had made a nice living for himself by having as few of these as possible.

Kahlil "Buster" Khan, Jr. struck an impressive pose. He was taller than his father and his full head of black, thick hair had not yet started to turn gray. Although not nearly as comfortable in formal business attire as was his father, we looked every bit the young successful man about Memphis. His photo was frequently on the cover of *Memphis Inc*, the monthly print collection of restaurant reviews and area advertisements published by the Better Business Bureau. He attended all but a very few of the business and society functions a company representative was called for. He didn't hate the life. He derived pleasure from the flirtations with young blonde women, and most of the functions served higher-end wines. And he loved the southern accents.

Buster had two loves in his life and neither of them had a thing to do with his father's company. He was a very much better than average golfer; Buster Khan also wanted to be a country music star.

Golf had come easily to him. He took great pride in the fact that he consistently posted rounds within a few strokes of par. He considered himself a naturally-gifted athlete. In truth, however, the many thousands of dollars his father had spent on private lessons probably had more to do with his level of play. Although Buster never took home the club championship at the prestigious and extremely elite Pinnacle Country Club, he placed in the top five almost every year.

More than golf, Buster loved country music. Not the twangy Hank Williams *Your Cheatin' Heart* country music. The new rage around Memphis and Nashville was being fueled by younger men with shoulder length hair and tighter jeans. As a subconscious homage to the genre's past most of them still wore cowboy hats and western boots.

Kahlil Khan had spent twice the money on guitar lessons as he had at the golf course in an effort to sharpen his son's ability to play. The money should have been spent on soggy okra soup for the homeless. Not that it was wasted entirely; Buster could easily change smoothly between the four chords he commanded. He simply never progressed beyond this.

Buster accepted his guitar playing limitations. Plenty of big names in the industry had achieved a level of stardom by writing and singing great songs. The cities of Memphis and Nashville were filled to the bursting point with high quality musicians of every sort. Buster's path to glory was to be in his ability to craft and perform moving and meaningful songs.

The legend Danny O'Keefe wrote meaningful songs

from birth. As has been the case with almost everyone else in the history of song-writing, the initial offerings are cliched and made of pulp before morphing into more profound and textured productions. This last phase of development, the morphing into something even marginally good, never happened along the musical trail traveled by Buster Khan.

The first time Buster wore boots into the conference room for the weekly management meeting Isabel noticed immediately. She was learning much about the owner of Kalkan; first and foremost, among his idiosyncrasies was an unbending mandate that proper business attire be worn at all times. If Isabel popped into the office after a Saturday morning workout to finish some report that was due the following Monday, she learned quickly to put on a suit and dress shoes. Each time she needed to visit the office on the weekend, she encountered Mr. Khan roaming the bottom floor where the station's employees were situated. He was gracious to those he encountered, and he always thanked them for doing such a great job.

When Khan entered the conference room the afternoon Buster debuted the new footwear, Isabel waited with heightened interest for the old man's response. Surprisingly, there was none. At the end of the meeting, however, when Allie, Malcolm Crawley and Buster rose to leave, Mr. Khan raised a finger toward Isabel.

"Please stay with me for just a moment, Isabel," he said from the head of the table.

"Yes, sir. Of course," she said as she reclaimed her seat.

When the others had left and Crawley had uncomfortably

closed the door behind him, Khan looked up from his reports and stared at Isabel.

"Did you see Buster's shoes?"

"Yes, sir, I did."

"What did you think of them?"

This was skating on thinning ice. Isabel had learned of Khan's predilection toward knee-jerk and completely out of proportion reactions and wanted to provide the perfect answer. Earlier that month Isabel learned first-hand how easily and without remorse Khan could alter someone's universe.

The caller ID on her phone was one she didn't recognize. The area code was from Mississippi, but this caller was one she did not know.

"Isabel Storey," she answered.

"Isabel, it's John Champagne. You got a minute?"

John Champagne was the station manager at an AM FM operation in Biloxi. He had the dubious honor of trying to make a go of it at the very site of Khan's initial foray into the business. Despite the fact that advertising dollars across the country were stampeding from radio and print to television, the Biloxi properties continued to perform within budgeted numbers. But only by very slim margins.

"Sure, John. Where are you calling me from? This number isn't programmed into my phone."

"I'm calling from home. Is your door shut?"

"Hold on," she said. A few seconds later: "it is now. What's going on?"

"So last night...well, this morning actually around two,

Mr. K calls me at home. I'm a little groggy, but I recognize the voice immediately."

"Wow. What did he want?"

"He asked what I was doing, and when I told him I was sleeping, he said he had something he wanted me to do with him. He said that he was on his knees praying, and that I should get on my knees and pray with him."

"Holy shit," said Isabel. She had known John Champagne from her first visit with Crawley to Biloxi. She liked him immediately. He was level-headed, honest and polite. She was also impressed by his high degree of professionalism. Of course, this characteristic was on display opposite Crawley's porcine inclinations, so it was an easy thing to pick up on. She had established weekly one-on-one phone calls with all the managers in Kalkan and she enjoyed her chats with Champagne more than most.

"So, what did you do?" she asked.

"Don't laugh, but I got out of bed and knelt down. My wife thought I'd lost my fucking mind."

Isabel smiled widely but was able to contain the chuckle she felt in her stomach.

"So, I tell him…OK, I'm on my knees now, Mr. Khan, what should we pray about? And he says: John, I'm praying right now that you can turn around the performance of the stations…you know that market was where I got my start."

"Yes, sir. And I'm honored that you have entrusted the operation to me. I truly am. And he says: Good, John, let's pray that we can increase the bottom line so that our Heavenly Father can make sure you keep your job. Shall we pray for that, John?"

"Oh my gosh," said Isabel. "What did you say?"

"What do you think I said? I told him I was praying the very same thing right along with him. That I would do my absolute best not to let him or our Heavenly Father down."

"That's about the weirdest shit I've ever heard, John."

"Wait. It gets better," said Champagne. "Malcolm Crawley called me about an hour ago. I've been fired."

After a few seconds, and when Isabel Storey became aware that her mouth was wide open, she offered condolences and support in her friend's unexpected job hunt. By this time in her tenure at Kalkan she had earned the title of Director of Operations. She was hopeful that a word from her to a possible new employer might help her friend.

With this type of somewhat erratic behavior as a backdrop, Khan's employees maintained a safe amount of trepidation whenever they interacted with him. Back in the conference room, the recollection of John Champagne's demise fresh in her memory bank, Isabel processed the question about Buster's boots. Clearly, Mr. Khan did not approve of them, or he wouldn't have asked. Of greater interest was that he had asked her to stay and discuss his son's fashion statement.

"Mr. Khan, you asked, so I'll tell you. I think the boots look good on him. In my opinion Buster is a striking young man. Also, in my opinion, I'm not sure I would wear them in our workplace. I take pride in the fact that we represent you in how we act and what we wear. And I can't see you wearing cowboy boots to the office, sir."

Khan processed this. He ran a hand through his oddly-colored and sparse hair.

"You get it. How we dress is important. It's a building

block. I want you to talk to Buster. He doesn't work for you but tell him that I am of the mind that all of us...everyone in my operation to some degree... answers to the Director of Operations. Position it however you want to, Isabel, but tomorrow morning the boots are gone."

"Got it," she said.

As she left the conference room and headed downstairs to where all the offices except Mr. Khan's were located, she wondered why he had selected her to relay this message. If anything, she would have thought Crawley would be the bearer of bad news. He had history with both kids. They clearly understood his position in the company hierarchy. She knocked on Buster's door keenly aware that some sort of transition was taking place. Only the old man upstairs, however, could provide details as to what that end game would look like.

"Buster, this might be a bit of an awkward situation, but your father asked me to talk to you about something."

"It's the goddamn boots, isn't it?"

She nodded without losing eye contact. Buster was smiling like a kid who'd been caught trying to take an extra jellybean out of the jar.

"I figured he wouldn't like them. Curious, though, as to why he sent you to tell me and not Malcolm. Some sort of changing of the guard?"

"No. No. No," she said holding both hands up. "I think your father trusts me...for that I'm very grateful...and he probably knows that Malcolm has a lot on his plate."

"We'll see," said Buster.

Isabel took in the room. Its walls were plastered with

Employee of the Month awards; the shelves were crowded with small and large golf trophies.

"You win all these trophies?"

"These are the big ones. I've got lots more in my den at home, but these are for the big tournaments I've won."

"I knew you were a golfer but didn't know you were this good. It's impressive, Buster."

Buster pushed his chair back and placed his feet on the desk. Isabel knew with certainty that the boots would be gone in the morning. This was a mild discharge of testosterone from a spoiled child.

"Just a suggestion, but why not wear the boots only when you're not going to be around your father?" she said.

"Yes, ma'am," he said.

As she pounded away towards her thousand calories on her favorite elliptical machine at the gym that night, Isabel ran a quick newsreel in her mind of the developments at Kalkan. In a couple of short years, she had been named Director of Operations, had clearly earned the respect and trust of the owner, had positioned herself as an equal to Buster and Malcolm Crawley, and had developed a solid friendship based on the guise of mentorship with Allie. She had also, despite enormous misgivings and loud warning bells, begun to have a minor romance with Mr. Khan's personal secretary.

Roberta Bertolli was tall. She had short black hair, dark eyes and an angular face. Not athletic, she had a thin body that spoke more to comfort than allure of any kind. She was thoughtful and supportive of Isabel from the jump. What began as Saturday afternoon beers and wings at a sports bar became weekends together once or twice a month. They did some traveling, they attended a few concerts and, on special occasions, went out drinking at one of the few gay clubs either of them knew existed in the greater Memphis area. Sex was an afterthought, but once that line was crossed, they both smiled more often.

"We'll both be fired if anyone finds out about this," said Isabel. They were sitting on the sofa in the living room of Roberta's apartment. Arby, a nickname comprised of her initials, had cooked shrimp and grits for Isabel. They had enjoyed dinner, had a couple too many glasses of wine and had settled into pleasant conversation in front of the television.

"Nobody's going to find out," said Arby. "We're friends, good friends, that's all. These people wouldn't know gay if it bit them. So long as we keep this to ourselves there is absolutely nothing to worry about."

Isabel kissed her and ran fingers through Arby's short hair.

"If you say so. You know better than I do."

Work with Allie was an exercise in patience. Khan's youngest child genuinely wanted to contribute to the success of her father's empire. She very willingly spent many hours in the conference room with Isabel reviewing profit and loss statements and performance metrics for each of the properties. She stayed late most nights reading reports and studying market trends. A big day in her development was when she realized that the long list of receivables she and Isabel were reviewing represented people who owed the company money and not the other way around.

"I get it now," she said to Isabel as she tapped her head with her right index finger.

Allie was a nice woman; Isabel liked her and genuinely wanted to help her grasp the concepts. On a couple of occasions Allie invited her to Wednesday evening church service.

"Thank you, Allie, but no thank you. I hope you understand that it's just not my cup of tea."

"It's not for everyone," said Allie. "I'm very entrenched in my church. It gives me sustenance and fulfills me. I couldn't be whole without it. But I understand."

To Isabel's thinking Allie dedicated her life to the company and to her church. She apparently did not date and rarely spoke of anything other than numbers and salvation. She was an attractive woman with dyed blonde hair and a predilection towards the heavy application of makeup. Allie never uttered a bad word.

This Friday night was special for Allie. She left work early and went home to shower and change into black leather pants. She drove her white Mercedes to a shopping mall close to her home in the hills and parked near the entrance to the food court. She sat with the engine running and looked straight ahead.

The boy who opened the back seat door and slid in looked to be of high school age. He wore jeans and a hooded sweatshirt.

"Good evening, Miss Allie," he said.

"Where did you park?" she asked.

"Outside of the sporting goods store. I didn't see anyone I know."

She drove in silence to her house and pulled into the garage. The garage door closed, she got out of the car and opened the backseat door.

"Downstairs. Now please."

While her guest was moving to the basement, she filled two glasses with ice water. She walked slowly down the steps to her laundry room making certain that her descent was being heard.

The boy had removed all of his clothes and stood in front of the dryer facing her as she entered. His penis was erect. The scene that followed this night was unchanged from that of previous nights. Allie placed his hands in restraints and connected them to a hook in the rafter above him. She tied a scarf over his eyes. She collected a small suitcase from a shelf behind the washer.

She opened a folding chair and sat three feet in front of him. The glasses of water were placed on the floor beside her. She opened the small case and removed a riding crop and a King James Bible.

"Now, let's begin."

The next hour was spent with Allie reading passages of scripture and the boy repeating them. When he faltered, as she knew he would, he was directed to turn away from her. The stinging swats with the riding crop were, she knew, very tolerable and left only slight markings on the cheeks of his ass.

With the evening's lesson completed, the boy was released from his constraints and the blindfold was removed. Allie had taken off her leather pants and the red silk panties selected specifically for this evening and sat, legs open, on the folding chair.

"Now, come over here and pray with me," she said.

He knew from many previous nights with her that he was now to kneel on the pillow she'd placed between her legs and perform cunnilingus.

"You make Miss Allie feel good, and I'll let you touch your dirty, disgusting worm and pleasure yourself," she said.

Thirty minutes later she drove him in silence back to his car.

"Thank you, Miss Allie," he said as he was leaving.

"Have a blessed evening," she said.

Buster played his guitar almost every night of his life. Convinced that his future as a singer-song writer was right around the corner, he worked hard at mastering the tunes he'd already written. Over and over, he played them in a sequence established to keep an audience listening with attentive ears. When the muse struck him, he was always prepared with pen and paper to capture the magic. Not for many years had he attempted to learn anyone else's song.

He was pretty sure that he was going nowhere with the name Buster Khan. Although born and raised in the southeastern United States, he carried with him a slight tinge of an Asiatic exotic. Boots and a hat would help; the name certainly had to change.

Zach Breeze and the Tornados came into being on a Friday night in Buster's basement recording studio. His three fellow musicians…the Tornados…loved the name.

The band was made up of men with day jobs. They could play, two on guitar and another on drums, but the city of Memphis trailed only Nashville and Austin as an epicenter of the highest quality studio musicians on the planet. The Tornados enjoyed meeting at Buster's every other Friday night. More than the comradery and quest to produce good music drew them there; Buster paid each of them two hundred dollars a session.

"Buster, we should think about playing out somewhere," said Eddie the drummer.

"Maybe," said Buster, "but you need to remember to call me Zach when we're playing."

"Sorry, Zach. You know, there's an open mic night at this little place I know right out of town a few miles. It might be fun to try out your songs there. A couple beers. You know? And it's small…no pressure."

The band discussed taking the show on the road as if they were planning a world tour. A van would have to be rented, equipment not provided by the club would have to be acquired, clothing was a consideration.

"I like the idea of dressing individually," said Walt the lead guitar player. "I mean, you don't see The Eagles dressing in costumes."

In the end it was Zach's decision.

"I want us each to wear jeans, boots and hats. Whatever kind of shirt you want to wear is up to you. If you need some cash for boots and a hat, let me know."

Buster called the club Eddie had suggested the following Monday.

"We're going to need about forty minutes to play our set. If that costs a little more, just let me know."

Later that day Buster sent the club owner a check for five hundred dollars. The date was set for the following Saturday night.

Isabel joined Allie and Arby at a table in the cafeteria on the first floor of Kalkan's office. Each of them had brought a salad from home.

"So did you hear the big news?" Arby said to Isabel.

"I did not," she replied while chewing.

"Tell him, Allie," said Arby.

Allie swallowed her lettuce and sprouts.

"Buster…well, Buster and his band are playing a mini concert this weekend. At this little club just on the edge of town. I don't think I've ever seen him this nervous. Except maybe on the golf course in some big tournament."

"I knew Buster was a musician, but I didn't know he was this accomplished," said Isabel.

Allie and Arby ate their salads in silence. They had both had the pleasure of hearing Buster play and sing. At a Christmas party three years earlier, the owner's son had been the entertainment portion of the evening. Attendees clapped politely after each song. Almost to a person, they approached Mr. Khan following the performance to tell him how absolutely thrilled they were to have been able to hear his son's music. Khan, who had groomed his namesake to take over the company one day, smiled with a closed mouth.

"We should go," said Arby. "The three of us should drive over and support Buster. It'd be fun."

"I could drive," said Allie. "I don't drink, so I could be the designated driver."

Isabel had misgivings about the whole thing. She enjoyed spending time regularly with Arby. Arby was smart, she enjoyed many of the same activities as Isabel: hiking, cooking, nice wines, exploring tiny towns in the area.

Although their sex together was not, as Isabel would have described it as over-the-cliff, it was enjoyable.

But Isabel wondered about mixing fun and work with the owner's daughter. That coin had two sides. In the end the enthusiasm of her two lunch mates won her over.

"Let's do it," said Isabel. "Let's go get us some country music."

Arby pulled her Honda into a visitor space at Isabel's apartment complex. In moments Isabel descended the steps from her second floor home. As discussed, both women wore jeans and sweaters. Arby had opted not to wear a bra.

"Nervous?" said Arby.

"About what?"

"This is our first outing together with anyone we know. Aren't you a little nervous?"

Isabel played with the radio.

"I'm looking for some shit-kicking country music to get us in the mood. And no, I'm not nervous. And, trust me, 'outing' is not the word to be using in that sentence."

"I think it will be fun," said Arby. "I've never seen Allie in a social setting. The Christmas parties, when we still had them. But those don't really count."

"Why did the parties stop?"

"Mr. Khan used to have the managers flown in with their wives. It was a huge event. A few years ago, a couple of them got out of hand a little…had way too much to drink. There was a scene. Some pushing and shoving. That was more than Mr. Khan could take. No more parties."

"What happened to the managers?"

"Malcolm Crawley fired them both the following Monday."

"I think we should have them again. Maybe just for the employees in Memphis. It would be fun, and it would do a lot for morale," said Isabel.

"You going to ask Mr. Khan?" said Arby as if daring her.

"Hell no," said Isabel, "but I bet I could get Allie to."

"He'll say they cost too much."

"This company makes a shit ton more money than it ever has," said Isabel.

"I've worked for Mr. Khan for almost ten years. Trust me, the more money he makes, the cheaper he gets."

Arby parked on the road in front of Allie's house. It was a two-story brick home with a two-car attached garage. The lawn was landscaped impeccably.

The two women walked across the front lawn and rang the bell. Allie emerged wearing the jeans and sweater uniform. She had added to the outfit with a pair of black cowboy boots.

"Wow, nice footwear," said Arby.

"Buster got them for me. He wanted me to look authentic tonight."

The women piled into Allie's Mercedes; Isabel took the backseat.

"I love your car," she said.

"Thank you, Isabel," said Allie. "One of the perks of being the owner's daughter, I guess."

"I don't know about that," said Isabel. "You certainly work your tail off around that place. I can attest to that. You probably earn this car many times over."

"Amen to that," said Arby.

Allie drove with eyes straight ahead. She was older than each of her passengers and out-ranked them at work. She could well have been offended at the not-so-subtle obsequiousness Arby and Isabel had just breathed her way. But she wasn't. Over a decade of attempting to join the club and just, by only this much, failing to make the cut had softened her to such platitudes. She was at a point in her life where she almost believed them.

The three Tornados were on the small stage when the women entered the club. The band-members wore matching hats and boots.

"Let's sit over there near the front," said Arby. "We'll want Buster to see us. It'll give him a lift."

"I wonder if he's nervous?" said Isabel.

"I talked to him this afternoon," said Allie. "He was excited, but I don't think he's nervous anymore. This is what he's always wanted to do."

The women sat at a small table. Within moments an extremely thin waitress appeared to take their drink order. She wore jeans that seemed to be sprayed over her skin. Her shirt was cut low, and she was not wearing a bra. A discount-rate tattoo of yin and yang was on her left clavicle. The lines between light and dark had blurred considerably.

Arby and Isabel ordered beers; Allie had a Sprite.

"How about you, Allie?" asked Arby. "Any musical aspirations?"

Allie exhaled almost in a snort.

"If you heard me sing, you'd run for cover. Buster got all the musical ability in this family, that's for sure."

"What do you do for fun outside of work?" asked Isabel.

"Well, like I mentioned, I'm very involved in my church. I think there's a good chance that I'm going to be asked to sit on the board. I also teach Sunday bible school. I'm very strict."

Isabel scanned the place as they waited for their drinks. The Tornados had apparently brought along some friends and family to beef up the normal Saturday night crowd. Well over fifty music lovers sat drinking and chatting as they waited for Zach Breeze to join his band on stage.

The club was dark and dusty. Photographs of famous country stars hung on each wall. Smoke lingered in the air but did not completely replace the faint aroma of processed cheese.

As the waitress was placing their drinks on the table, an extremely overweight man dressed in khaki slacks, shirt and sport coat took the stage. He had a long ponytail that appeared to grow out of the baseball cap he was wearing. He was sweating profusely under the spotlight directly overhead.

"Ladies and gentlemen," he said taking the microphone out of the stand in the center of the stage. "Thank y'all so much for being here tonight. We have a special treat for you on Open Mic Saturday this evening. It's a new band in town, and they've picked our place to try out some new music. Let's treat 'em right. Up first tonight, here's Zach Breeze and The Tornados."

"That's actually a really good name," said Arby amid the smattering of applause.

Buster smiled widely as he stepped up on to the stage and strapped his guitar on. He wore the obligatory boots and hat, but he wore them comfortably, something that could clearly not be said for his bandmates. His white shirt had mother-of-pearl buttons and was pressed as parchment paper.

He strummed his guitar once and placed his hand on top of the microphone now returned to the mic stand in front of him.

"Thanks very much for the warm welcome. We're glad to be here and we hope you like our songs."

The music was about as diverse as one would expect from a repertoire created with four chords. The Tornados actually held together pretty well. At a very minimum, people in the crowd could tell that the songs had been rehearsed over and over again.

Buster's singing voice was neither strong nor weak. He carried a tune and enunciated his lyrics. A few of the folks in the audience continued to chat while the band played, but not many.

"My pickup truck, it needs some luck, the empty seat's for you," went over well.

As did: "I'm drinking Scotch whisky in hopes that it drowns out the sweet, sweet taste of your smile."

"That girl done nabbed my heart," elicited some minor giggles, but none reached the stage.

When they had finished the last song of their set, Buster thanked the crowd for coming. He introduced The

Tornados. The applause originated from some parts of the floor, but not all.

Buster placed his guitar in the stand on the side of the stage and joined his sister and two fellow-workers at their table.

"Buster, that was really great," said Arby as he slid an empty chair from the next table to theirs.

He raised his hand as he sat.

"Please, Roberta. While I'm performing, I need you to call me Zach."

"Well, Zach, I'm impressed. How do you feel?" asked Isabel.

"I think it went well. We could have been a little tighter in some areas. But all in all, I'm pretty pleased. Thank you for coming, by the way."

"Do you need some help with your equipment and instruments?" asked Isabel.

"No thanks. That's part of the job of The Tornados. They'll clear it out for the next performer."

Zach declined a beer with the women. He thanked them again for showing up and supporting the band. Before he left the bar, he chatted briefly with the owner.

"Come back any time," said the big man.

Zach removed his hat as he slid into his Mercedes. It was a warm night. He drove out of the lot with his windows down. He could just hear the band of four high school boys beginning to cover a Steely Dan song as he drove away.

The Tornados loaded their instruments and equipment into the van that Buster had rented for the occasion. They tossed their hats into the back before joining the family and friends who remained seated in the bar. Beers were ordered. They discussed the set of songs.

"We need to tell Buster that he should make an album. Go to Nashville. Hang out for a couple weeks. We could get paid what those studio guys get."

The Tornados were realists. As they chatted, the high schoolers on stage were performing songs far more complex than anything Zach's band could have handled. All the same, they knew a meal ticket when they saw one.

"We'll pitch the idea at the next practice."

It had been six months since the hotel episode with Crawley the night Zach and his band launched their bid for stardom. Isabel reflected on the clearly illegal activities she had devised as she, Arby and Allie sipped their drinks and listened to the high school Steely Danners.

Shad had been raised by very decent, very middle class parents in central Ohio. Although not church-goers, Bob and Betty Storey had done their best to raise a young woman of integrity and kindness.

She had excelled through high school and college and was universally accepted as a trustworthy friend.

Her rationalization as she lay in her hotel room bed that night several months ago was simple: Crawley started it. She could have added to this thinking. She could have considered that her career was potentially limited at having to work for such a pig. That she had to look out for herself. That her reputation was besmirched because of where, and with whom she was associated. That she did all the company's heavy lifting and earned a pittance compared to Crawley and the kids. But none of that was necessary as she began to formulate a plan those months ago. In grade school playground tomboy logic, it was simply enough that Crawley had started it.

Of enormous help was the fact that Mr. Khan trusted her. She had replaced Crawley as his right hand man; she performed due diligence on properties he was considering, she fired the managers whose prayers to keep their respective jobs fell on Deaf Ears, she ate soggy vegetables at Ginny's once a week and talked growth strategy.

It also helped that the others occupying offices on the third floor of the building were ineffective. Buster was far too immersed in his potential music career to even go through the motions of caring about Kalkan. Crawley spent more and more of his time out of the building. Arby had shared with Isabel that Khan was aware of Crawley's outside interests, but that he was not ready to make any big changes yet. Allie, of course, tried. She arrived at the office early and stayed late. She poured over reports. She picked Isabel's brain.

"I didn't realize that Allie grew up on a farm."

This from the Ford dealership manager in Pensacola the night he and Isabel had dinner after work. It was on one of her grand tours of the properties, an exercise Mr. Khan fully endorsed. Bobby Nixon had very recently joined Kalkan. He was a native of the Florida panhandle and ran a tight ship. Isabel liked his easy-going demeanor.

"You got me on that one," she said. "I don't believe Mr. Khan ever owned a farm. Not his style at all."

"No. No," said Bobby. "They obviously lived on a farm.

I'm pretty sure Allie was kicked in the head by a large animal at some point in her childhood."

Isabel smiled but did not laugh.

"Amusing," she said, "but you have no idea how hard she works, how hard she tries. If you put half of the energy into your job that she does into hers, you'd be employee of the year. Not a big deal, Bobby, but let's show a little respect."

Chastened, he went back to talking inventory and finance rates. Exchanges like this, although not common, made the employees of Kalkan look up to the five foot six inch woman who always seemed to be on the clock. Managers talked to each other, and the high degree of professionalism that Isabel projected was well known throughout. She was a whiz at numbers; her ability to see through fluff when reviewing budgets was known widely throughout the company; she could manage the difficult decisions with men twice her age when necessary. But above all else, Isabel Storey demanded professionalism.

And then there was Mr. Khan. For over three decades he had built and operated the empire. Six hundred employees, several dozen corporations, each with separate loan agreements and accounting systems. He read reports on money coming in and money spent to operate the businesses for long hours into the night. Years ago, he'd had the small office adjoining his renovated into a bedroom of sorts. It was not uncommon for him to remain on the fourth floor through the night. The day after his wife died was the only time employees at Kalkan could remember him not in his office. A day later, of course wearing a light-colored suit, shirt and tie, he started a new streak.

The attention to detail and a leaning towards micromanagement had taken its toll. Khan was creeping up on 85, and the once razor-sharp mind had begun to dull.

Arby, who sat in the small entry area outside Khan's office, shared more with Isabel than was probably appropriate.

"He calls the same managers multiple times a day and has the same conversations with them…gives them the same directions."

Isabel nodded but did not comment.

This was the landscape. Once Isabel decided to put a plan in place there would be no luck involved in its success. In a corporate environment more professionally-operated, she never would have been able to try something like this. Of course, Isabel Storey, seemingly always one step ahead of those around her, would never have tried in that environment.

It started with leg work. Lots of leg work.

Isabel collected the necessary paperwork to establish several dozen corporations. Each named her as the individual tied to the company. This was problematic she knew, but the forms called for a name and social security number. If the shit ever hit the fan there would not be a whole lot she could do. She had begun to develop an exit strategy but leaving before she was ready was a last option. She also consulted with an attorney to get an idea as to what kind of jail time came along with theft the nature of which she was planning.

"I know someone at work who is talking about doing this," she said.

"Depends on the amount of money," said the woman in the gray suit. "But it could be five to ten, easy."

She guessed that the State of Tennessee employees processing these documents would not go to the trouble of verifying physical addresses, so she drove around Memphis selecting vacant lots for each company's home office. The State, she knew, would only send mail once a year at renewal time, and by that time she could be close to gone.

Then began the arduous task of opening post office boxes and bank accounts, one for each company. It was important that each mailing address have its own zip code, so Isabel spent a week of vacation driving within a 100 mile radius of her apartment painstakingly setting them up.

Groundwork in place, it was simply a matter of starting.

"Mr. Khan wants me to do a tour of the properties ahead of schedule."

Isabel was sharing this with Crawley, Buster and Allie. They were seated in the third floor conference room as she filled them in. This had become standard operating procedure immediately following her one-on-ones with Khan. None of the three had any inclination to visit Khan's office unless they needed to. They were, however, keenly interested in what he had to say to Isabel.

"I was going to make my normal tour in a couple months, but he wants me to see if their prepared for Y2K."

"Y2K is almost irrelevant," said Crawley. "Almost nothing in this company is computer dependent. I've been begging the old man to let me set all that up, especially the various inventory systems, for years. Y2K will be a non-factor for us."

"Agreed," said Isabel. "So should I tell Mr. Khan that I don't need to go?"

Crawley had stopped entertaining any thought of calling Isabel's bluffs long ago. He was making a lot of money for very little work at Kalkan. He knew the day was coming when someone, probably Isabel, would replace him. But that day would not be anytime soon; he had no interest in questioning Khan's decision.

"Go," he said. "Don't do anything I wouldn't do."

"I want to invite all of you to go along with me," said Isabel. "Mr. Khan didn't mention that it was mandatory, but we've got some new management faces out there. It might be good for them to be able to put faces to names."

Isabel knew good and well that this invitation would immediately be declined.

"I've got bible school," said Allie.

"I'm in the early stages of forming my band," said Buster.

"Busy," said Crawley.

That evening Isabel mailed out the first invoice. It was to the car and truck dealership in Pensacola in the amount of $5,500. In the memo box, she typed: *Y2K K. Khan.* She calculated mail and processing time and scheduled her visit to coincide with the first time the dollar amount would show up on the operation's payables report.

Over the course of the next several weeks she repeated this process. Firing off invoices, scheduling flights and hotels. There were a lot of properties. She was going to be a busy girl.

The first conversation with Bobby Nixon could have been a script for those to follow across the Kalkan empire.

"What's the $5,500 for Computiks?" she asked.

"I don't know. We never heard of them."

"May I see the invoice please?"

She noted that it had something to do with Y2K preparedness and that it had Mr. Khan's name in the memo box.

"I have to call him in a bit anyway," she would say. "I'll ask."

In the end, she assured Bobby Nixon that Mr. Khan had hired Computiks.

"I believe we finally convinced Mr. Khan that he needs to get away from all this manual book-keeping. Computiks, I guess, will be rolling out this process over the next several months. Just put my initials on the invoices when you get them."

It was that easy. Bobby Nixon asked no questions, and he certainly had no desire to speak with anyone in the corporate office…specifically Kahlil Khan. Many of the other managers throughout Kalkan had been hired by Isabel. A few had not had a moment's contact with anyone but her. And none of them were responsible for tax filings to outside companies. This was Isabel's job.

Computiks, Digital Commerce, Business Graphics and all of the other corporations Isabel had created fired out monthly invoices and received monthly checks in their assigned PO boxes. The checks were deposited into each company's bank account. Checks from each of these accounts were deposited in one master account three blocks from Kalkan's headquarters. Of interest, none of the corporations would appear adjacent to another regardless of how the data was sorted. If the names and numbers were ever consolidated into one accounting entity, the separation of names, addresses and zip codes that Isabel had established precluded all but a professional and detailed audit from ever making a connection.

Nine months into her exercise Isabel had deposited a touch over 800,000 dollars into her main account. To a person, the managers throughout the Kalkan empire had not mentioned the Y2K invoices after her initial discussion about them. Buster was in a deeply creative period of song-writing, Allie was swimming in spreadsheets she still did not quite understand, Crawley made only token appearances in the office on meeting days and Khan had kept busy reading profit and loss statements.

"He reads these reports, and some of them are years old," Arby was telling Isabel after work one night. "He doesn't know."

Isabel had driven to Arby's apartment after a ninety minute workout. Arby had picked up Chinese food and arranged the containers, place settings and a bottle of white wine on her dining area table.

"Thank you for dinner," said Isabel as she expertly ate Szechuan pork with chopsticks. Arby used a white plastic fork.

"You want to do something this weekend?" asked Arby. "It's supposed to be nice. Maybe we could go to that B and B in the mountains. Eat some barbecue."

"Listen," said Isabel, "I need to talk to you about something."

Arby put her fork down and looked up.

"What's up?"

"This is no fun, but I think we need to cool down this relationship a little. I worry about the whole work and play thing. I think we need to take a little break. Maybe just for a while."

Arby's eyes teared, but she did not cry. She was a woman in her thirties living and working with people who, had they known who she was, would not have approved of who she was. She had had three lovers in her adult life, and Isabel Storey was by far the kindest, most attractive and most fun.

"I'll miss your eyes," she said. "And your hands."

"I'm sorry, Arby. Let's just see, OK?"

After a few moments of silence, Isabel got up to leave.

"I think I should probably head home."

"Here," said Arby, "take your pork. We don't need to feel like shit on empty stomachs."

As Isabel drove toward her own apartment, she mentally checked the box of disentangling with Arby. She liked Arby a great deal, enjoyed her company and her sense of humor. She liked the comradery and the confidences. She worried, however, about implicating her friend in the event the get-rich-quick plan currently deployed throughout the company went south. In the unlikely event Isabel was caught, Arby, she figured, could profess ignorance without lying. Isabel also planned on a quick exit when she sensed the time was right. It was one thing to hurt someone she truly liked by ending a relationship; it would have been something much worse to simply disappear.

As another early step towards departure Isabel had created one last company, Genesis Engineering, and had opened a bank account and credit card under that name. It would be easily traceable to her, of course, but only if whoever might be looking cared to turn over a rock or two in doing so. Her intention upon leaving Kalkan and Memphis was to use her name as seldom as possible, at least for a good long while.

Six weeks later Isabel's phone rang. She was sitting in her office looking at a map of the United States. It was Arby's extension.

"Hey, Arby."

"Hi, Isabel. Hey if you have a few minutes, Mr. Khan wants to see you and the kids. Could you grab them up and come up to the conference room?"

"We'll be there shortly."

Allie was immediately up and out of her seat. Buster had to remove the boots he had been wearing and replace them with a pair of brown oxfords.

"What's he want? Do you know?" asked Buster as they rode up to the fourth floor.

"No idea," said Isabel.

"These little impromptu meetings with daddy are usually fun," said Allie.

Khan sat at the head of the conference room table. Arby sat to his left and held a note pad on her lap.

"Good morning," said Khan. "How's everybody today? We running the company the best way we can?"

"Doing our best, Mr. Khan," said Isabel.

"I know you are," said Khan. "The deposits I'm seeing across the board are running pretty high."

This was an accurate depiction of Kalkan's finances. The company was making more money than ever in its history.

Khan had bought a stake in the NFL team recently awarded to Memphis, and his flagship television station was selling in-game ads at incredibly high prices. Additionally, Crawley had convinced Khan to invest in cable television as a hedge. After Isabel had selected a target market and performed the due diligence necessary to secure financing, the new enterprise became a cash cow. As icing on the cake, the outside properties were running at record-setting margins. Kalkhan was spinning off over ten million dollars a month in net profits.

What worried Isabel was that Khan seemed aware of all of this. She had banked on his inability to remain aware of the company's minutia. She was of the mind that he was reading year-old performance reports. She took cold comfort in the fact that he had the same conversations with the same people multiple times a day. But now she was not sure. Nobody had given this empire to this man. He built it with his own energy and with his own money. He was a millionaire a couple hundred times over, and he had not procured these riches by being foolish or fooled. Uncharacteristically, Isabel felt a trickle of sweat under each armpit.

"I want to talk about Isabel," Khan began. "I want to talk about what she's been doing."

Isabel's face was frozen. She wanted desperately to make eye contact with Arby but knew she couldn't. Allie sat with a straight spine and took in every syllable. Buster re-tied his shoes.

"She's been working her rear end off for the company, that's what she's been doing. We're having the best year of our existence this year, and most of that is due to her. Isabel, well done."

She smiled without knowing she was smiling.

"Believe me, sir, it's a team effort."

"Not anymore," said Khan. "As of this moment, Isabel, I want you to know that I have replaced Malcolm Crawley with you. You're the new Senior Vice President of Operations and he's gone. The first woman to achieve this, young lady. Congratulations."

Isabel sat stunned. Arby had shared with her along the way that this might transpire, but Isabel had taken those statements with grains of salt...a naked Arby lying beside her in bed could embellish with the best of them.

For the first time since putting in place the plan to make herself rich, Isabel had a tinge of misgiving. She thought of what she had done, she thought of her parents, she thought of Khan doing the right thing with Crawley.

"And as a reward for all your hard work, Isabel, you'll be getting a five hundred dollar bonus at the end of this year. And your pay will be increased by one and a half percent starting with our next pay period."

"I'm overwhelmed," said Isabel. "Thank you, Mr. Khan. I won't let you down."

"Lunch today for everyone," said Khan. "On me."

As Isabel descended to the third floor with Khan's children, she kept in the smile she felt. Another meal of soggy vegetables to digest, a few more months of invoicing and trips to her banks, and just a while longer of maintaining the image of company warrior. She could do that standing on her head. But for now, she needed to get back to the map in her desk drawer. She had a trip to plan.

The last spot on the map Isabel had pointed her number two pencil to was the small town of Sault Ste. Marie, Michigan. It sat at the most eastern point in that state's Upper Peninsula. The town had a small college, a large Native American presence, several middle-scale restaurants and a bustling, four month-long tourist business. Isabel had vacationed there as a young girl with her parents.

As she drove her rental car up from Detroit on her reconnaissance mission, she passed through a good number of towns and cities. It would turn out that many of them… most of them… possessed greater charm and ambiance than Sault Ste. Marie. Better restaurants, more upscale shopping, far better architecture. The one thing all of these other communities lacked in comparison, however, was the reason she had flown from Memphis to Detroit and was now driving five hours straight north. The bridge connecting Sault Ste. Marie, Michigan to its sister city of Sault Ste. Marie in Ontario, Canada was two miles long and crossed the St. Mary's River. In ten minutes, give or take, Isabel Storey could be in another country.

As she drove into town there was little to impress her. The main street was made up of banks and bars; the primary side street paralleling the river consisted of unspectacular restaurants and shops selling low priced souvenirs.

She drove the rental through the main section of the Native American reservation and was impressed with the neat and tidy rows of duplexes. The tribe had built a hockey stadium, three schools and a casino with adjoining hotel.

After checking in to her motel, The Waterview, she walked the streets and eyed the tourists. She was very young the Summer she and her parents had visited, but she had slide show photo images to call upon. The big boats, the Fudge Shoppes, the water seemingly everywhere.

She bought the local newspaper and went into the Water's Edge restaurant. The waitress was a fleshy young woman of twenty or so. She wore a necklace made with a bear claw.

"What's good?" asked Isabel.

"Pretty much everything," said the young woman. "But we're kind of known for our fish."

"How do you prepare it?"

"Any way you want it. Fried, broiled, pan-fried."

"How do you get it?" asked Isabel.

"Fried, of course."

Isabel ate her fried fish with a baked potato as she read her newspaper. For a small town daily, it was not at all bad. Heavy on local sports, shipping schedules and advertising, it was well written and laid out carefully. Of main interest to Isabel were the classifieds.

As the country approached the year 2000 the economy was percolating. Cost of living tended to follow the up-tick; everything, it seemed, was costing a bit more.

This development had not, however, transpired in the real estate market of remote sections of the Upper Peninsula. Isabel had no intention of buying a house of course, but there were plenty of them at very reasonable prices if she changed her mind.

The next morning Isabel drove around the area and checked out a few of the locations that listed houses for rent. She was still a few months from jumping but wanted to get a lay of the land.

It was a cool and crisp Friday morning. The tourists

cramming into restaurants and shops represented the last wave of the season.

Isabel opened a checking account at a small bank claiming to be locally owned and operated.

"I'd like the account to be in the name of my company. Genesis Engineering."

"Where can we send your checks, Ms. Storey?"

"Actually, I won't need them for a couple months. How about I pick them up when I get back?"

She crossed the International Bridge into Canada. At the guard booth on the other side, she was asked if she had any firearms or alcohol. Her interviewer was wearing a shirt and tie. His jacket was green and adorned with a small, red maple leaf on each shoulder. He told Isabel to have a nice day as he waved her through.

She ate lunch in a bistro on Queen Street in the city center. When asked by her waiter, a tall and thin young man doing his best to grow a mustache, if she wanted a second glass of wine with her soup and sandwich, she declined.

After crossing the bridge back to Michigan and answering the same questions at the border patrol booth, she went to her motel room and took a nap. Her flight to Memphis was the next afternoon, and she didn't look forward to the five hour drive to the Detroit airport. This, however, made her smile. If she dreaded the chore of getting all the way up to Sault Ste. Marie, so might anyone with any interest in following her.

Isabel's workload under the auspices of her new title did not increase. She had been doing Crawley's job for months. In actuality, it was easier for her with him gone; she no longer had to carry on the charade that she was including him in any decisions. When Khan asked her if she'd like to move into Crawley's old office, she politely declined. A cleaning crew wearing HAZMAT suits and armed with nuclear powered disinfectant would be necessary before she willingly took over that space.

As she continued to almost single-handedly run the empire, Isabel began the process of disengagement from the company and the community. She gave a three month notice that she was breaking the lease at her apartment. She contacted a church in her neighborhood and made arrangements to donate every bit of household furniture, linens, dishes and utensils to a family in need.

"If I may ask, are you moving some place where you can't take all this with you?"

This was from the white haired volunteer woman taking down Isabel's contact information.

"I'm getting married and moving to Texas," said Isabel.

She was not certain which lie was less likely to ever happen.

Two months into the new year Isabel fired off the last of the invoices. Within 30 days she had received the last of the payments. It took a couple vacation days, but she visited each bank and closed all of the accounts. The PO boxes would remain open until they were not renewed.

Her main bank account around the block from Kalkan headquarters now held just under two million dollars. If anyone cared enough to notice, a reasonable question might be what the hell did Genesis Engineering do?

But in the business world, that amount of money was

not eye-catching. It was certainly enough, however, to change Isabel Storey's life.

She stayed late in the office scrubbing the accounting lists of the fictitious companies she had created. There was still plenty of historical documentation: cancelled checks, payment records, copies of invoices. But this documentation rested in the filing cabinets in the external operations. No tax information had been processed from the Kalkan headquarters, so Isabel felt marginally comfortable that the people who would be taking over the company's day-to-day business would move merrily forward and try their best not to look back.

"Arby, I need a few minutes with Mr. Khan."

This was Isabel talking to her friend and former lover.

"Let me put you on hold for a second."

Isabel looked around her office. Never one for opulent displays of trophies and trinkets, she had packed the few pictures and gifts given her into one small box.

"He said to come on up," said Arby.

A few minutes later, Isabel surprised herself by being nervous. She nodded at Arby as she passed through to Khan's office.

"Good morning, Isabel. How are we doing today? Please..." he said, motioning to the chair across from him.

Isabel sat and crossed her legs. The note pad and pencil she always brought with her were absent.

"Mr. Khan, we're doing quite well. I know you see the same reports I do, and I'm very pleased with our performance right now. There is one thing, though. I need to tell you that I'm leaving the company. I'm leaving Kalkan."

Historically, when people left the company, it was not from their own decision. Khan was not practiced in dealing with voluntary departures. His background was firing people. He sat trying very hard to figure out what to say.

"Mr. Khan, you need to know that I have truly loved working for you, and that I am very grateful for everything you've done for me. It's just time to move on for me. Some of my reasoning is personal."

As Isabel spoke, she sat higher in her chair. Her hands unclasped. She felt herself moving to higher ground.

"Is there something I can do to keep you, Isabel? A raise?"

"No, sir," she said. "I've made up my mind on this and I hope you will respect that. I do want to mention that I think Allie has come a long way. I'm not sure what your plans will be to replace me, but she might well be able to assume a lot of my responsibilities."

Khan sat in silence. Isabel was pretty sure that what she had just said had not registered, that it would come back to him later. Isabel knew that having Allie in charge of just about anything would further muddy any trail she might have overlooked.

"Thank you for everything, Mr. Khan."

She stood and exited the large, overly-decorated office, being certain to close the door behind her.

"I just quit," she told Arby before heading to the elevator.

"Jesus, why?"

"Time to move on, Arby. Sometimes it's just time to make a change."

"When's your last day?"

"We're living it."

Isabel stepped behind Arby's desk. She bent over and kissed her very warmly. The spearmint taste of Arby's tongue lingered for a moment as Isabel stepped on to the elevator.

"I love you, Arby. You're wonderful."

Within minutes, she had placed the box of her belongings into the already packed VW sedan and driven off the lot for the last time.

1968

Norman Tall Tree was the first male member of his family to learn to read and write. As a nine year-old, he would sit for hours and read to his younger brother Peter. The books, all three of them, came from the nuns at St. Matthew's; they were not lengthy, but the boys were young enough to enjoy them with each reading.

That year, when Norman entered the fourth grade at public elementary school and Peter the third, their father died. Walter Tall Tree had given very little other than his name to the boys. A man who lost every battle ever fought with a strong desire to drink passed away at the age of thirty-four to issues associated with a destroyed liver and a crippled pancreas.

The boys did not miss him. Their lives were unchanged. Walter had never been much of a provider, leaving the financial burden of keeping up their small, rented house to his wife and the kind parishioners at St. Matthew's. Their mother worked six days a week as a fry cook at a department store in town. The boys ate grilled cheese sandwiches and wore pants and shirts handed down from Catholic boys who had outgrown them.

They were adequate students but failed to fully invest

in the normal activities of elementary school. Children who fend for themselves from early ages often swap the need for life's niceties and tender loving care for self-reliance. Their mother was firm and loving; she simply had miniscule deposits of energy to spend on the boys at the end of her days. She would make them dinner before soaking in the tub until the water was cold. Often, she went to bed before they did.

There were other boys from the tribe at school. Norman and Peter sat together on the bus rides and kept to themselves. The other boys were loud and required constant shouts from the bus driver to settle down. Many of the other boys had baseball gloves in the Spring; in Winter, they could pack a snowball tight as ice and throw it with high velocity; they injected a smattering of bad words into their speech. The Tall Tree boys were not certain that the words they were hearing were evil; they simply associated them with their dead father and wanted nothing to do with them.

Each Sunday morning their mother would wake them in time for a cup of hot chocolate before all three of them would make the mile trek to St. Matthew's. As often as not, some kind-hearted parishioner on the way to mass would pick them up.

"Meet us here after mass, Mrs. Tall Tree, and we'll give you a lift home."

The boys knew this to be life. They remained quiet unless together and alone. They anticipated silent kindness from those around them. They sat in church, one on each side of their mother. They sang hymns with atonal, high-pitched little boy voices. They behaved.

"I want to be an artist," said Norman.

He and his brother were sitting at the kitchen table with their mother. It was a Sunday evening, and they were eating tuna fish casserole, a gift from one of the women at church. It was enough food to feed an army, their mother had said. Although the boys never went to bed hungry, they often were close to that edge. Sitting with straight spines and napkins tucked into the tops of their shirts, they ate with serious intentions.

"I think that's wonderful," said Mary Tall Tree. "What kind of artist?"

"I like to draw," said Norman. "Mrs. Pentangelo says I'm really good at it, too."

"That's wonderful. Why don't you draw some pictures tonight and we'll put them on the refrigerator?"

"We don't have any magnets," said Norman.

"You draw the pictures. I'll get the magnets. And what about you, Peter? What do you want to be when you grow up?"

"I think I want to be a soldier."

"Well, there's no reason you boys can't grow up to be those things. Just do your homework and pay attention in school."

That evening, after the remains of dinner had been wrapped up and placed in the refrigerator and the dishes washed, dried and put away, Norman and Peter changed into pajamas. They brushed their teeth and said their prayers before climbing into the bed they shared. Quite often they would share aspirations in whispers. This night, however, they lay silently listening to their mother. She was in her own bed and could not appear to stop coughing.

The boys had no real family to take them in when the cancer that had stalked their mother finally won.

"Who will take care of us?" asked Norman the week before she died.

She had gone downhill rapidly since the night of the coughing session. By that time, the disease had taken a good hold on her. Had treatment options been available in the small hospital in Sault Ste, Marie, they would not have been presented to an Indian woman living fully over the edge of poverty. There was the issue of payment, but there was also the issue that Mary was too far along the path to death by the time she was diagnosed.

"I spoke to someone at the church," said Mary Tall Tree.

Never a fleshy woman, she had thinned to under 100 pounds. Her fingers were bones with skin wrapped loosely around them. Her black hair was pulled into a ponytail, making her face seem even thinner than it had become.

She was propped up in her bed and rested on the extra pillows the boys had brought from their own bed.

"We don't need them," said Peter. "We never use them anyway."

The boys were standing at her bedside. Children their ages should feel many things, but never among them should be terror. Norman held his hands together as if in prayer. Peter, already taller than his older brother, looked everywhere other than at the bed holding his mother.

"There's a big house in another part of the state where children who have lost parents can go live until a nice family is found to take them in. So, you boys might get to go on a trip."

"But this is our house," said Norman. "All of our stuff is here. Our school."

"I'm sure you can take a lot of your things with you," said Mary Tall Tree. "I'll tell you what…tomorrow morning when the woman from the state comes over with Sister Teresa, we'll talk to her. I know it's frightening, boys, but it will work out fine."

Norman bent at the waist and placed his head on his mother's lap. Her bony hand ran through his short black hair. He cried.

Mary swallowed with difficulty. The promise she made to herself not to cry in front of her boys was desperately close to being broken.

"You boys will be OK. Just take care of each other. God won't allow anything bad to happen to you."

Peter walked quietly out of the room and put his snow boots and jacket on. He did not zip the coat before exiting the little house, and the cold air went through his chest and wrapped around his heart. He walked down the street towards the playground adjacent to St. Matthews school. It was a bitterly cold evening. His tears froze instantly to his high cheek bones.

The boys were billeted with a parish family the last few days of Mary's life. She lay dying in a hospital bed, and they very clearly could not remain at home. Will and Edie Kelly, an aging couple whose own children had grown and gone, smiled with tight lips as they welcomed them. Norman and Peter were polite and silent. They ate and drank only what was presented to them at mealtimes. For the first time in their lives, they slept in separate beds. Before falling off to sleep they whispered fears to each other instead of the usual plans for what they were going to be when they grew up.

The parish ladies had bought them new shirts and slacks for the funeral and for the trip to the Indian Orphan Home 250 miles away in Marquette where they would be driven after their mother's service. Each boy was given a large suitcase, and a nun from the Catholic school drove them to their house to collect what they could for the trip.

"What will happen to the things we don't have room for, Sister?" asked Norman.

"I'm not certain," she said.

In actuality, she was very certain. The owner of the house would now rent it out as a furnished home; the personal belongings of the Tall Tree family, those items that would not fit into the suitcases the boys dragged from room to room, would be donated to this charity or that.

"Let's hope that whatever you boys don't take with you will go to some children worse off than you," she said. "Make sure you each pack up a picture of your mother."

The priest performing the funeral mass asked each person in attendance to pray for the two young boys Mary had left behind. A small number of pews were occupied with friends and with men and women Mary had worked with.

Before ending the service, the priest approached Norman and Peter and placed one hand on each head.

"Dear Lord, please hold these boys in Your hand and protect them. Please provide a good family to take them in and raise them in Your light. And please guide our church in our efforts to bring them back among our loving family."

After the service, the suitcases already loaded into the

trunk of Will Kelly's car, the boys climbed into the back seat and waited to be driven to their new home. It was cold and cloudy. They sat with their winter coats zipped up to their chins.

"That was a lot of talk about our family," said Norman. "I didn't think we had a lot of family. That's why we're going to live in a home a long way away for children like us, right?"

Peter stared out the window at the small gathering of people who had been at the funeral. He knew that they would soon be eating cake and drinking coffee at the reception the priest had mentioned would immediately follow the service. He was glad that he and his brother did not have to attend. He was glad that he and his brother did not have to pretend that any of these people were his family.

"Fuck," he said.

He was not entirely sure of the word's meaning, but it was the worst thing he could think of saying, and it needed to come out.

No one ever referred to the home Norman and Peter were driven to by its proper name. The Diocese of Marquette Home for Native Children instead was called the Indian Orphanage. Even the boys and girls living there called it that. They were Indians. It was an orphanage.

By the time Will Kelly pulled into the drive it was beginning to darken. Days are short in Winter at that latitude, and he faced a long drive home. A kind man, he had spent the first hour of the trip attempting to engage the boys in conversation. He told them what he knew about the orphanage; he sprinkled in amenities that he hoped would be available. Norman asked about art supplies, and Will

Kelly assured him that they would be in abundance. When Kelly asked Peter what he wanted to do for fun at his new home, there was a non-committal, but polite response.

As Will Kelly parked the car, the boys peered eagerly out the back-seat windows at their new surroundings. They noticed someone standing on the large porch at the front of the house. She wore a heavy parka with the hood pulled up over her head and was waving hello to the car. The snow boots that protruded out the bottom of her black habit were made of fur and were light brown.

The woman walked down the steps and was at the back seat window before the car had come to a full stop. She smiled with perfect teeth and dimpled cheeks.

She opened the door on Norman's side and leaned in.

"Hello, Norman. Hello, Peter. Which one's which?"

"I'm Norman. This is my brother Peter."

"I'm Sister Collette. Welcome to our home. Let's get inside and have a cup of cocoa."

The nun shook Will Kelly's hand forcefully; she carried one of the suitcases up the steps and into the little office that sat off the side of the entryway.

When the boys had removed their heavy jackets and taken seats on the red sofa off to the side, she sat behind her desk.

"Mr. Kelly, are you driving home tonight, or staying in town?"

"No. I'll be heading back, Sister."

"Well, we certainly thank you for bringing Norman and Peter to us. They're in good hands, Mr. Kelly. You don't need to worry about them."

"Of that I am sure, Sister."

"Boys, do you have anything you want to say to Mr. Kelly?" she asked.

They thanked him in unison.

As he stood in the doorway, Will turned to the nun.

"Sister, we'd have loved to take the boys in. We just are a little old and a little tired. They're so young. They need more than we feel we can offer."

"You're a very kind man, Mr. Kelly. The boys are going to be fine. Pray for them, as I will for you."

When Sister Collette returned from walking Will Kelly to the door, she sat in a chair facing the boys. She hunched forward, elbows on knees, and looked intently back and forth from one set of dark eyes to the other. Only her face and green eyes were uncovered from the black habit.

"Before we get our cocoa and show you where you'll be sleeping, do you have any questions? I know you must be a little confused and a little frightened, but I want you to know that you boys are my friends. I will do everything I can to help you."

"I have a question," said Norman.

Sister Collette turned slightly so as to face Norman head-on.

"Yes, Mr. Norman."

He had never been referred to that way, and it made him smile.

"Do we have art supplies here?"

"Oh, yes. And there are lots of art supplies at the school you boys will be going to. I didn't realize you were an artist. How exciting for us to have you here."

For an instant, but only for an instant, the fear of uncertainty that had been eating into his belly vanished.

"And what about you, Mr. Peter? Any questions?"

Peter shook his head before stopping and looking up into the woman's eyes.

"How long will we live here?"

Sister Collette now turned directly to the younger brother.

"That's going to depend," she said. "Your church back in Sault Ste. Marie is trying to find a family that will provide a good home for you. I think they're trying to see if you have any relatives they might not know about. So, the answer to your question is that I don't really know. What I do know is that we're very glad to have you here, and I think you're going to do very well. And this will be your home until we can make sure that you'll be safe and well-taken care of somewhere else."

The second floor of the house had been renovated into two large dormitories, one for boys and one for girls, each with a bathroom. There were six single beds in each dorm. The unclaimed beds that Norman and Peter would occupy were on opposite ends of the room. It was as far apart as they had ever slept.

The day had been long and filled with emotional turns and twists. The funeral, the long car ride, meeting Sister Collette and the boys and girls they would be living with. The sheets on their beds were laundered and stiff. The boys slept without moving, as if still sharing a bed.

In the morning, there were rituals. After dressing, beds needed to be made, pajamas put away, teeth brushed, faces washed. Norman and Peter Tall Tree had grown used to the bowl of cereal waiting for them on the table at home; the hot breakfast of scrambled eggs, sausage links and toast was an extravagance they had seldom enjoyed.

"I wonder if this is such a nice breakfast because it's Sunday?" Norman asked his brother.

They were sitting side by side on one of the eight foot long benches in the kitchen dining area. The table was throat high on each of them. A bowl of steaming eggs and a plate of toast were placed in the center of the table for the event any of the boys wanted seconds.

The girls' table was arranged in a mirror image, taking up the other half of the room. Three girls on each side wearing identical white blouses and black, mid-calf-length skirts.

The walls of the dining area were decorated with pictures of Jesus and the pope.

"We don't get sausage every day, and sometimes instead of eggs we get oatmeal. But it's Sunday. Sunday meals are the tits."

The explanation came from a taller boy across the table. He wore the same white shirt and black pants as the other boys, but he wore these clothes differently. Walter Crow was older, his voice was deeper, he would perhaps think about shaving soon even if he had no need to.

The Tall Tree boys ate with napkins tucked into their shirts. They chewed their food with closed mouths. When Peter had wanted another piece of toast, he asked the other boys at the table if that would be alright.

When breakfast was finished, each boy and girl carried their dishes and silverware into the kitchen adjacent to the room with the long tables. The children stood in a line and waited their turn to scrape their plates and deposit silverware and dishes. An older woman with a noticeable mustache and multiple chins collected the items and prepared the large sink for washing.

"Usually, two of the girls handle the dish-washing," said Walter, "but not on Sundays. Mrs. Scumaci handles it on Sundays. She also does the laundry."

The miniature bus that carried all of the children and Sister Collette to church that day was waiting in the parking lot the following morning. The orphan children were lined in the foyer of the house, each wearing their heavy coats and carrying a book bag. The Tall Tree boys had never owned a book bag. Norman slung his over his shoulder as if it held something heavy instead of simply air. Peter carried it in his hand as if it were a briefcase.

The bus was driven by the caretaker of the church. His name was Cameron Tootoo, and he was an extremely youthful-looking man in his early twenties. He was Indian, and he had taken over all the gardening, minor repair and maintenance duties for St. Bartholomew's when he graduated from high school. By that time, he had spent over half of his life at the orphanage. As caretaker, he moved into a single room apartment attached to the rectory at the back of the parsonage that housed the fathers. It was simple, but his new home had its own bathroom and a private entrance. He took most of his meals with the bishop and the other priests. He was, for the most part, a no-nonsense bus driver. Once in a while, however, he would delight the children by zooming down the only hill on the way to school.

"I think we're out of control again," he would shout to the riders in the back.

Even Peter began to smile at these episodes.

Nellie Redford taught the fourth grade at St. Bart's. She had been out of college for six years and lived at home with her parents. She had been raised, and continued to be, a devout Catholic. She had dated a few boys on campus but was a bit of a loner. At school, she spent more time studying on Saturday nights than on socializing.

Teaching at St. Bart's, where she herself had been educated, was her dream job. An only child, she had a genuine love for children; the job also allowed her to serve her Lord. She also liked the fact that she was only one of two teachers not wearing a habit. She was an oddity at a Catholic school, and this pleased her.

Norman took to her immediately. She had blond hair that she kept short, just above shoulder-length. Her eyes were the color blue he could only duplicate by mixing watercolors. He did this on more than one occasion and delighted in showing her. Nellie Redford knew full well that boys developed crushes on teachers. It made her cautious, but it also made her smile. She had been briefed on Tall Tree recent history. She knew that the boys had lost both parents within months of each other. They needed some light in their lives; maybe she could provide it for at least one of them.

Although not much of an artist herself, Nellie was able to see genuine talent in Norman's artworks. He was an average student in all other areas, but he displayed ability well beyond that of any of the other children in class. When Nellie had the children sketch their own hands without looking at the pencil touching paper, Norman's drawing had come alive. The other boys and girls gathered around his desk to admire his creation. He was the only Indian in the class, he thought to himself, but he was the best at drawing a picture. At least a hand.

"All the great artists in history have done this exercise," Nellie told her students. "Any one of you could grow up to be famous, you know?"

A pudgy girl standing beside Norman's desk raised her hand.

"Yes, Melissa," said Nellie Redford.

"I think Norman's going to be the only one of us to be a famous artist."

"Perhaps," said Nellie. "That's very nice of you to say, Melissa. Now, let's take a look at our science books. Art's over for today."

Nellie Redford watched closely as Norman Tall Tree put his art belongings into his box and slid it beneath his chair. She watched him open the lid of his desk and remove his science book. He was smiling to a degree that made his eyes close to slits. She saw this and it warmed her.

Peter Tall Tree did not possess his brother's gift for creating pictures. Ten months younger than Norman, he was a slightly lower than average student. Already the taller of the two by several inches, he kept to himself unless engaged by someone else. When Norman would step through the portal into his artistic outlet, Peter would sit quietly and look out the window. He had a fondness for the outdoors, and always volunteered to do the shoveling after it had snowed.

The first week of March the temperature climbed into

the forties. For children growing up this far north, it was sub-tropical. It energized them. Their blood flowed more freely. They stood straighter. They spoke more rapidly.

The six boys on the bus traveling from St. Bart's back to the orphanage that first day of thawing snow ranged in age from eight to fifteen. They were planning on playing basketball after changing out of school clothes. They expected some snow to still cover the parking lot where the hoop stood but looked forward to being outdoors. Teams were chosen as Cameron Tootoo drove carefully along.

Tootoo stopped Peter as he was exiting the bus.

"Peter, wait here a minute. Let these other boys off. I want to ask you something."

Peter stepped aside into the front row seat and stood as the other boys filtered past. The oldest boys always seemed to gravitate to the seats furthest back.

"Let me ask you, do you like to fish?"

Peter stood holding his bookbag. His black hair had begun to grow out and lay straight on his forehead and over his ears. His dark eyes darted to the basketball hoop and back to Cameron.

"I went fishing with my father once, before he died. He kept yelling at us to keep quiet. He was drinking a lot of beer. It wasn't very fun."

"Did you catch anything?"

Peter shook his head.

"Listen, if the weather stays nice like this, how about you go with me one of these Saturdays? I know some good spots, some streams where we can catch some trout maybe?"

"Can Norman come?"

"Let's just you and me," said Cameron. "Norman has stuff to do. It'll be good for you to get out of the house a bit."

"I'll have to ask Sister Collette," said Peter.

"OK, but we already talked about it."

"OK, then," said Peter as he stepped down from the bus. He greeted Sister Collette as she walked past him to the bus. He was in a hurry to get inside and change for the game.

"How did that go, Cameron?" she asked from the bottom step of the school bus.

"We're going fishing, Sister. I think he liked the idea."

"Thank you, Cameron. Please be safe driving back to Bart's."

That night, after the boys had flung up shot after shot with an all but airless basketball and returned to the home with red cheeks and stinging hands, after dinner had been eaten and chores completed, after teeth had been brushed and prayers chanted, Peter Tall Tree climbed into his bed. He did not spend any thought on the distance that existed between his bed and his brother's, nor did he think of his mother waiting for him up in heaven. He thought only of fishing. He thought only of fish.

It rained and sleeted two Saturdays in a row, but this was followed by a sunny and warm weekend. Cameron drove into the lot in a blue sedan. When Peter climbed in beside him, he saw fishing rods in the back seat.

"Whose car is this?" he asked.

"It's Father Gillette's. I better be careful with it, or he'll excommunicate me."

Peter nodded.

They drove into town and toward the big lake. Cameron turned onto a gravel road that paralleled the shoreline, and then again onto a sand road consisting of two tire tracks with scrub grass separating them. There was a small pull-off about a half mile in. He parked the car.

They grabbed up the fishing gear and lunch box and walked a trail for a hundred yards and came instantly, miraculously, upon a stream flowing swiftly towards the lake.

"Here," said Cameron. "Let's see what kind of damage we can do here. This spot's been pretty good to me."

Cameron showed the boy how to bait his hook with worms. Skittish at first, Peter completed the task with nonchalance within his first few tries.

"A little later this Summer this stream won't be so full. When we fish it then, we'll be able to see the trout a lot clearer. For now, just pick a spot you think is good and lower your line in."

The day was productive, the highlight being when Peter caught a good-sized trout. He had remembered what Cameron had told him. Be still and wait for that feeling in your fingertips as you held the rod. Then... not too hard, not too soft... snap the end of the rod straight up to set the hook.

"You're a natural, Peter," he said. "That was awesome."

Peter forgot that he was supposed to be a sad boy who had lost both parents. He could not wait to get back to the home and show Norman his fish.

When they had returned to the car the light was beginning to fade and a chill had started to creep towards them from the big lake to their north. Cameron gingerly turned Father Gillette's car around and inched it along the sandy road. As they neared the gravel road that would take them back towards town, they were hailed by two older men walking the road. Each carried a shotgun slung over a shoulder. Both wore flannel jackets.

The smaller of the two men raised his hand as if stopping traffic at a busy intersection. Cameron crept the car to a stop and rolled his window down.

"Where you boys been?" asked the man who had stopped them.

"Doing a little fishing," said Cameron.

"Catch anything?" said the same man.

"We did. I got lucky and got a few; my friend here got his first fish. A nice trout."

"You boys got a license?" asked the larger man.

Cameron's hands remained on the steering wheel. He smiled wide.

"We're both Indians. Full blooded. We don't need a license."

"Well, isn't that just fucking great for you then?" said the smaller man.

"Take care," said Cameron. "We have to be going."

"See you later, Tonto," said the larger man.

Cameron Tootoo drove slowly away. He fought the urge to peel out and leave the men in a cloud of sandy dust. But they had guns, and it would not have been the right kind of lesson to impart on his fishing partner.

"Those men were not nice," said Peter.

"They were not, but maybe they couldn't help it. Maybe we should pray for them."

"Right," said Peter Tall Tree. "Right."

On sunny Spring mornings Nellie enjoyed the walk from her parents' home to the school. She carried a huge purse slung over one shoulder. Graded tests, a brown bag containing her sandwich and fudge brownie, keys and pens and pencils represented just about her entire life. Her parents had often told her that she was naturally pretty, and that wearing makeup was not needed. With the exception of a small tube of lip balm to prevent chapping, she didn't own any.

She loved the church. It had been built in the early 1900's and possessed a gravitas that many of the newer buildings lacked. The stained glass alone was awe-inspiring.

Adjacent to the church separating it from the school of the same name was a large garden. Nellie could not name many of the flowers and shrubs that grew there each year, but she enjoyed sitting on the benches and eating her lunch when the weather cooperated. Her fellow teachers, the nuns, seemed to avoid the outdoors. Nellie had always assumed that to be cloistered was a lifestyle for them; they were programmed to remain indoors.

On a certain Wednesday of abundant sunshine and fifty-five degrees Nellie walked to work. She noticed Cameron Tootoo working in the garden. He wore green overalls and big work boots covered with mud. He was turning over soil with a hoe. It appeared to be a strenuous job. His shoulders snapped back with each release of dirt from the earth.

He stopped as she walked along the edge of the garden separating the church and school.

"Good morning," she said.

"Good morning, Nellie," said Cameron.

She smiled quizzically and tilted her head slightly to the right.

"I know I've seen you everywhere around here," she said, "but I don't remember that we've met. At least not formally."

Cameron Tootoo smiled a wide smile with straight, white teeth.

"Well," he said, "I don't really do anything formally. I know your name from school. You were a few years ahead of me. And I've seen you coming and going here. And at mass sometimes. I'm Cameron Tootoo. I keep up the grounds and maintenance of the church. I been here a few years or so."

"And you drive the bus from the orphanage," said Nellie.

"Yup. That, and I run about a million errands a day for the fathers and Mrs. Baker."

"Well, it's nice to formally meet you, Cameron. You've got your work cut out for you with this garden I can see,"

"It's my favorite project," he said. "I like seeing people sitting in here who appreciate it. I like working with the ground. I like being outside."

"Well, I certainly enjoy it. I eat my lunch out here quite often. When the weather's nice."

"I know you do," said Cameron.

Nellie felt her cheeks warm. She looked at Cameron's face and caught, just for a moment, the darkness of his eyes. His cheekbones were pronounced. His skin was brown. His hands were rough and caked with mud. He smiled again.

"I guess I should get in to work," she said.

"I hope you enjoy your lunch in my garden," he said. "Maybe I'll see you again sometime."

The next morning was dreary. Although not raining,

clouds lay low in the sky and threatened to spit rain at any time. The temperature had dipped ten degrees.

"Give me a minute, Nellie, and I'll give you a lift to school on my way to the shop," said her father.

"I think I'm going to walk, Daddy. It doesn't look too bad out there this morning and I need the exercise."

The flirtations lasted through April and into May. Nellie walked to school on days that would have kept a commercial fisherman at home; Cameron tended to the garden as if it were Versailles. They waved to each other at the beginning of mass on Sundays and chatted on the steps after the service had ended.

On a Tuesday in the second week of May Cameron asked Mrs. Baker for a sandwich.

"It's a beautiful day. I think I'll eat in the garden."

"Yes. Yes," said Mrs. Baker.

She was a large woman who perpetually wore a dusting of flour on her hands and apron. She had raised six sons with her husband Tom. She knew boys like she knew pie crusts.

"Yes, Cameron. I think you need to spend a little more time in your garden."

He was not certain, but he believed he saw her wink.

Nellie sat on the bench facing east. Her blond hair had grown out a couple inches. The daily walks to and from school had given her a confidence in the way she looked. She was more toned; she took strides along the sidewalk rather than steps.

"Deep in thought?" he asked as approached her.

"I'm not ever too terribly deep in thought, I have to admit," she said.

"May I join you?"

"Sure," she said. "It's your garden after all."

Cameron sat as far away as possible on the bench. He unwrapped the sandwich Mrs. Baker had given him and took a large bite.

"Turkey sandwiches," he said. "Mrs. Baker cooks a turkey once a week. The fathers love it, and she says its cheap."

"PBJ," said Nellie with a mouthful of sandwich, "the building block of any good school lunch."

She had packed two chocolate chip cookies and gave one to Cameron. She drank hot tea out of the screw-top cup of her thermos. She wanted to offer Cameron a drink but thought that such an offer, drinking out of the same cup, might be forward.

"Would you like a drink of my tea? It's still pretty hot."

He turned to look directly at her. He smiled that wide smile with those perfect teeth.

"I'm good but thank you anyway."

"I don't have cooties," she said smiling back.

"No, I don't suspect you do."

Nellie finished her cup of tea and screwed the cap back onto her thermos.

"Well, I suppose I should be getting back to my kids. Their lunch will be over soon."

"Hey, Nellie, before you go, I want to ask you something."

She turned to face him without saying anything.

"If this is awkward, just tell me, but I was wondering if you might like to go out to a movie some night."

"Like a date?" she asked.

"Like a date. Except you'll have to drive. How pathetic is that?"

"That would be lovely, Cameron. I'll look forward to it."

She had retained eye contact throughout the entirety of his invitation and her own acceptance. Something about how deeply dark his eyes were made it hard for the shy woman teaching the fourth grade at St. Bartholomew's to look away.

The movie was a western. Outnumbered but terribly brave, the ranchers defended their homes and loved ones from a marauding Indian band. The little girl with blond pigtails was saved only by the crack shot of the ranch hand who plugged the Indian in the back just as he was about to perform some grisly act.

"I'm embarrassed about that movie," Nellie said as they walked the three blocks to a diner. "I mean, the stereotypes, they've got to bother you, don't they?"

"I don't want to say you get used to them. I think you get kind of numb to them. It's not a big deal. I'm really glad that you came out with me tonight."

They sat across from each other in a booth in the back of the diner. They drank hot tea, Nellie with nothing added, Cameron with sugar and cream. They ate warm apple pie with thinly sliced cheddar cheese on top.

They reminisced about going to school at St. Bart's. She told him about life at college. The words that passed from mouth to mouth across the table were not fashioned to impress anyone. Nellie and Cameron sat comfortably, each more intent on listening than taking a turn speaking.

"Tell me about living at the orphanage. I wonder has it changed much from the time you were there to now."

"I don't think so. It's still very structured. The nun who runs it now, Sister Collette, she's wonderful. Very warm. Almost like a mother to those kids."

"Was she there when you were there?"

"No. This old nun, Sister Thecla, she ran the place. Not an ounce of motherhood in her, let me tell you."

Nellie smiled. She sipped her tea and ate the last crumbs of her pie with her finger.

"Was it difficult for you?"

Again, the smile.

"What you have to remember is that for most of the kids that go there, the orphanage is an improvement over whatever their lives looked like before. I didn't, but a lot of them get handed around from this place to that before settling in at the orphanage. I mean, you know, you're a teacher. Kids flourish with structure. It's when they don't have it that they start to make bad decisions."

"You should be a teacher, Cameron."

"Maybe I will be," he said.

They walked slowly back to the car. The air was thick with silence as Nellie drove to Cameron's apartment at the back of the rectory. She parked in the church lot and looked straight ahead.

"That was fun," she said. "Thank you for asking me."

"Thank you for saying yes," he said.

She broke the next brief spell of quiet by asking him if he'd like to go out again.

"Isn't that what *I'm* supposed to ask?" he said.

"How about we divvy up those duties? I don't think it's a law that I can't ask."

Cameron smiled. Nellie's hands rested on the steering wheel.

"I don't know the timing involved in kissing," said Cameron. "I'm not sure if it's date number three or four. So, I'm going to count lunches in the garden as dates and call tonight number four."

Nellie sat frozen. She had been on dates with boys. Rarely, she had sat in cars kissing and fumbling with clothing. But it had never been the right time; it had never been the right boy. A breath of guilt had always seemed to flow through her at moments like these.

She turned and placed her mouth on Cameron's. It was not as smooth as she had seen in the movies, but it was the most comfortable kiss she'd ever had.

"I liked that," she said. "I want one more."

After they had said their good nights, after she had backed out of her parking spot and started to pull forward, she rolled down her window and shouted goodnight once more to her date. This was not the Nellie she knew. Then again, the Nellie she knew would not have asked for a second kiss.

And she could still see that smile finding its way to her in the dark.

It was a picture postcard kind of day with high interspersed clouds, a light breeze working its way the three miles from the lakeshore to the orphanage and a temperature that begged the Indian boys and girls to wear shorts and tee shirts. Peter was shooting baskets with Walter Crow. Walter was a gifted athlete. He played on the school basketball team in Winter and ran track in the Spring. Peter was almost as tall as the older boy but had not grown into his frame sufficiently to do much more than fling the ball awkwardly skyward. When he missed hitting anything at all with his shots, he would flip his long hair out of his eyes and smile.

Norman sat on the porch watching the boys. He had a sketch pad on his lap, a gift from Nellie Redford, and was working away at something.

These activities were interrupted by Cameron Tootoo as he pulled the small school bus into the lot and parked. He stepped down from the bus and smiled.

"Give me a shot," he said to Peter.

Peter passed him the ball, and Cameron aimed for several seconds before firing. The ball arced cleanly through the air and landed with a thud, having missed its target by over a foot.

"You're almost as bad as I am," said Peter. He laughed until tears came to his eyes.

"Come here," said Cameron to the two boys. "I need some help with something."

The boys followed Cameron Tootoo up into the bus. Peter's heart, he was sure, almost flew out of his chest as he saw the bicycles. There were six of them, varying in size and color. Peter prayed to his dead mother that one of them could be his. He inaudibly formed the word *please* with his mouth.

"Some rich guy at the parish did a good deed," said Cameron. "He told me to bring these out here and let him know how many more to ask him for if anybody who wants one doesn't get one. It's Christmas in July, boys."

Sister Collette and two of the other children joined the boys in the parking lot.

"Sister, some nice man at the church gave us these bikes," said Walter Crow. "He's going to send more if any of us wants one and there's not enough. Can we keep them? Please?"

The woman in black looked at Cameron.

"Everyone who wants one gets one?"

"Yes, sister."

"Well, I guess we can keep them. You boys will have to make some room in the shed out back. We can't have bicycles laying around the yard, right?"

The boys said 'yes, sister' in unison. It sounded like snakes hissing.

"Can I ride this one, Sister?" asked Peter.

He had selected a bright red model that seemed to fit him perfectly.

"No, you cannot, but you may," said Sister Collette.

The Tall Tree boys had been clothed their entire lives with hand-me-down shirts, pants and shoes. Even their underwear came from some anonymous boy who had outgrown it. Norman and Peter opened the two or three gifts donated by various church-goers each Christmas. On birthdays, their mother would bring home a cake purchased at the grocery store. The only bikes they had ridden were those of neighbor children who gave them a turn when they themselves were bored.

It took Peter a few trial runs before he mastered the gleaming red bike. Once he had recovered the hang of it, he raced up and down the road in front of the orphanage, his hair flying out from the back of his head.

"Don't go too far that you can't see the house," shouted Sister Collette.

Norman returned to the porch and sat in his chair. He opened the sketch book and flipped to a new page. His eyes went from his brother to the page and back as his pencil flew across paper. This boy on the bike, this gangly and boyishly inelegant person with whom he was growing through life, was smiling.

On their second date Cameron Tootoo and Nellie Redford ate pizza. They sat at a table for two with a red and white checked tablecloth made of plastic.

"Tell me about college?" he asked.

"It's not really much different than high school. The classes are a little more in depth. Even the people aren't that much different. You have students who really try to do well, like me. And you have kids who are just there because their parents want them to be there. And there are always some kids who just stay in the background. You really don't know who they are."

"That would be me in high school. You'd remember, but you were already gone when I got to the tenth grade."

"You calling me old, Cameron?"

"Never."

They walked hand in hand back to the church garden. They sat at forty-five degree angles on the bench and kissed.

"I don't know anything about you," she said. "Tell me how you came to be here. Tell me what you did and where you were before you moved to the orphanage."

"I'm from a tribe in northern Ontario. The rez is real close to a small town called Wawa."

"OK, don't be offended, but I think that's so cute. Cameron Tootoo from Wawa. It sounds a little like baby talk."

He smiled.

"I never thought of it like that, but you're right, it does."

"Okay, continue please. But first…"

Nellie kissed him again. She tasted pizza on his tongue and wondered if he could taste it on hers.

"Well, my folks died in a car crash when I was twelve. You have to understand that the people living there are really poor. Even if there was someone to take me in, they wouldn't have had the income to feed another mouth. So, this priest at the church up there, a really nice man named Father Flynn, he arranged for me to move down here and live at the orphanage. After high school, the caretaker at St. Bart's was retiring and I thought, 'what the hell,' why not give it a try. I've been here ever since."

"So, are you a Canadian citizen?" asked Nellie.

"No. My ma was actually born in the states, over in Wisconsin some place. I'm not really sure how my folks met. I had what they call dual citizenship until last year. Then I had to pick one, so I picked here."

"You ever go back to Wawa?"

"There's no reason to. I wouldn't mind seeing it. I remember some things about it. Maybe after I get a real job and start making some money. A person is not going to get rich working for a Catholic Church, you know?"

"But who will take care of my garden?" asked Nellie.

"Oh, It's your garden now?"

"You knew that all along, admit it."

It was dark, and Cameron could make out only a few of the features of her face. Her blue eyes looked dark.

"I am liking you a great deal, Nellie Redford."

"God, you are a handsome man," she said.

Then the world that was occupied by Norman and Peter Tall Tree shifted again. On a Tuesday afternoon, after they had ridden their bikes all the way into town and back, and after they had carefully placed them in the shed behind the main house, they were greeted by Sister Collette on the porch.

"How was the bike ride?" she asked.

"It was fun," said Peter. "But we're pooped, Sister."

She held in most of the smile; only a tracing across her lips escaped.

"Come in my office a minute before you get busy," she said. "I would like to talk to you."

The boys followed the nun and stood in front of her desk as she took a seat.

"Sit down, boys. I have some good news for you."

They silently took their seats across from Sister Collette; they sat still as stones and looked at her.

"You know how this home is here for boys and girls who have no one to look after them, right?"

The boys nodded in unison.

"Well, when the church is able to find someone who wants to look after our children...someone who is kind and is committed to helping raise the children in a loving home...well then the church makes arrangements for the children to move there."

"We don't want to leave here," said Norman.

His younger brother sat without blinking.

"Oh, my goodness," said Sister Collette, "but you don't know the people who are going to take you into their home. It will be a far better situation for you than living here. You really must give it a chance and go into it with an open mind."

Peter looked up and into Sister Collette's face.

"When do we have to leave?"

"Those arrangements are being made, but it's looking like it might be tomorrow morning."

"Where are we going?" asked Peter.

"Back to Sault Ste. Marie. A nice family in St. Matthews has offered to provide you a loving home."

"Do we get to keep our bikes, Sister?" asked Peter.

"I'll check," she said. "Now you boys should probably go upstairs and begin packing up your belongings."

"Yes, Sister," said Norman.

The boys climbed the steps to the second floor and walked without speaking to their respective beds. The suitcases each of them had brought to the orphanage had magically appeared on each bed.

The room was empty. The other boys were busy, scattered throughout the big house and the property surrounding it.

Norman loaded his art supplies first: brushes, his sketch pads, the tiny watercolor jars. He was hungry and wondered what Mrs. Scumaci was making for dinner.

"I wonder what kind of food we'll get at our new home?" he asked Peter.

Peter did not turn to face his brother. He did not speak. He continued packing neatly folded shirts, socks, underwear and slacks into the suitcase. The photograph of his mother rested on the bureau, and he took it into his hands. He looked at her face for several seconds. The unsettledness he had felt in his stomach returned after months of absence. It took away his hunger. It was cold and dark and as heavy as wet sand. It prevented him from moving his mouth into anything that resembled a smile. It hurt him.

"They're not going to let us keep our bikes," he said to Norman. "You wait and see."

That night, after the children were bundled off to bed and Mrs. Scumaci had left for home, Sister Collette sat at the desk in her bedroom. She had removed the belt made of rosary beads and the black clothing and now wore only a cotton nightgown. Her hair, a color light brown that only she knew, was clipped short.

"My Lord," she said into the quiet space of the room, "please watch over these boys and keep them in Your light. They are so precious and so vulnerable, and they are just beginning to find any confidence at all. You know all of this, Lord, but please hear my prayer and protect them. And blessings to the church and all who are associated with it. Amen."

The woman who had been known to friends and family as Laura turned off the lamp on her desk and tip-toed to her single bed. She lay calculating the events she knew were going to transpire in the morning. She contemplated, as she did on many nights, her decision to become a nun. She had been mostly successful at substituting any biological gnawing to have a child with the boys and girls for whom she was responsible. She loved each of them.

Laura was blessed and reveled in the light of her God and her church. She took enormous pride in the fact that she had dedicated her life in this manner. Her faith was profound.

But on this night the warming light eluded her. She lay in darkness and thought of the boys sleeping upstairs. The prayer she had just spoken came from someone else's mouth. Her sleep, on and off for the next seven hours, did not refresh her.

In the morning Sister Collette showered and dressed. She had grown used to wearing the black clothing. She could ice skate in the Winter and shoot baskets in the Summer without giving a thought to the floor-length habit.

Entering the kitchen to make a cup of tea before Mrs. Scumaci arrived to make the children their breakfasts, she was startled to find Norman sitting in the near darkness at one of the long tables.

"Good morning, Sister," said the boy. "Is it alright that I'm down here by myself?"

"Of course it is, Norman. Would you like a glass of milk or a cup of tea this morning?"

"Milk please."

She did not turn on the kitchen lights. The tiny light coming from the hood of the oven that typically remained on all night was sufficient.

Sister Collette put a kettle of water on to boil and filled a coffee mug with milk for Norman.

"Here you are, Norman," she said placing the mug in front of him. "Excited about your new adventure this morning?"

"A little. We like it here a lot, Sister. Even Peter likes it here, and he doesn't like it very many places."

This made the nun smile. She had watched boys and girls move through her universe for several years. She had seen them at their lowest, most vulnerable grounding. She had rejoiced at their recoveries and had wept at their failures to escape the darkness they often wore as they came to her. She stepped behind Norman and settled his unruly hair with her hand.

"Norman, this will be fine for you and your brother," she said as she moved back to the stove. "The church would not be arranging for this unless the people you're going to be with were kind and supportive. You must believe this. More important, though, is that you have to get Peter to believe it. You're the older brother. It's your job in the eyes of God to help and protect him."

Norman nodded solemnly. This was serious stuff for him. He had never felt as if he'd been given a job by anyone, let alone God.

"I'll do it, Sister, but Peter is usually the one protecting me."

The nun poured steaming water into her mug. She attempted to stifle the laugh she felt; it came out as a single exhalation.

"I'm going to miss your humor," she said.

Norman drank milk from the large mug. He had not yet figured out why his efforts at humor failed, but that his moments of seriousness made people smile. But this knowledge was not important at the moment. At this moment he sat very contentedly in the semi-dark kitchen and drank his milk. At this moment he felt Sister Collette's kindness brush against him as if it were carried by a warm breath of wind.

The big station wagon pulled into the lot shortly after noon. The boys and girls had just finished a lunch of sloppy joes and macaroni and cheese. Mrs. Scumaci and two of the older girls were busy cleaning dishes. The other children dispersed toward various chores and activities.

Norman and Peter Tall Tree had dragged their large suitcases down the stairs and had placed them in the foyer outside Sister Collette's office. They had dressed in their black slacks and white shirts at her request and had taken seats opposite her desk while waiting.

"Ah, here they are," said the nun as she heard the car tire's crunching gravel. "Let's go meet your new family."

With very slow movements the boys rose and followed her to the porch. There seemed to be less oxygen the further away from the door they stepped. The air moved in and out of their small lungs with an unusual rapidity.

The man who exited the driver's side door and marched toward the porch was short. He carried more weight than his frame was intended to accommodate, and his red hair was thinning. Baldness was in his immediate future. He wore dress slacks and a golf shirt; his black shoes looked right out-of-the-box.

The woman who followed him towards the porch steps was thin. She wore a knee-length dress with yellow flowers printed on it. Her hair was dark brown and was pulled into a bun. Despite the warm weather, she carried a white sweater along with a large pocketbook.

"Good morning, Sister," said the man as he neared the steps. "Mike Borman. My wife Barbara," he added tilting his head at an angle so as to identify her. "These the boys?"

He climbed the steps and extended his hand to the

nun. The firmness of her grip, equal to his own, took him by surprise.

"Yes. This is Norman and Peter," she said. "Won't you please come in and have a cup of tea as we say our goodbyes?"

Borman affected a look of seriousness. It was the look he deployed when being spoken to by the bosses at work; it was the look he rolled out when he feared the priest might be glancing his way at mass.

"Of course," he said. "Of course."

The Bormans, the nun and the two boys walked to the kitchen and took seats at one of the large tables.

"Mrs. Scumaci? Could you boil water for tea please?" asked Sister Collette. "Boys, would you like something?"

The Tall Trees shook their heads in unison.

"Speak up, boys," said Borman. "It's impolite not to answer."

"No thank you, Sister," said Norman. "We're fine."

The adults drank their tea out of large mugs and the boys sat in silence listening to the conversation filling the air around them. They heard Mike Borman tell the nun about working at a steel mill across the river from Sault Ste. Marie in Canada. They heard Sister Collette tell the Borman's about Norman's prodigious artistic talent, and about Peter's love of fishing and the outdoors. They heard not one peep out of Barbara Borman.

When finally it was time to leave, Peter looked at Sister Collette and raised his hand as if in school.

"Yes, Peter...you don't have to ask for permission to talk," she said with a smile.

"Are we going to get to keep our bikes?"

"Well, I think that's up to Mr. and Mrs. Borman," she

said. Then to Mike Borman, "the boys were given bicycles by a parishioner in town. Might there be any chance of taking them back with you?"

"We really don't have room, Sister. The back of the car is loaded with stuff. Let's leave the bikes here for some other children, and we'll see what we can do about replacing them when we get home."

"Well, that sounds reasonable, doesn't it boys?" said Sister Collette.

They trooped down the steps and into the lot. The boys dragged their suitcases and Mike Borman hoisted them into the third seat area of the big station wagon.

Before they climbed into the back seat of the car, before they set out on the newest leg of their young lives' journey and before they headed back to the town that had spit them out only a few months earlier, the Tall Tree boys were embraced. First by Mrs. Scumaci, then by the young woman dressed in black. It was the first time either boy had been held since the death of their mother.

"Alright, boys, in the car," said Borman.

As they pulled out of the lot and headed east, Sister Collette remained. She stood in the dust the car's tires had stirred up and watched the vehicle fade away into nothing as it drove out of her life.

"In Your hands now, Lord," she said. "Please."

Sister Collette, the woman otherwise known as Laura, went back inside and sat at her desk. She was uncertain if replacement children would be sent to her soon, or if there would be a time of two empty beds. What she was certain of was that they would be arriving eventually. All of them. And that she would be ready to welcome them in her nun arms and shower them in the kindness her God had granted her.

The car ride back to Sault Ste. Marie was a road map of days and months and years to come. Mike Borman pontificated. He gave the boys the rules of the house. He mentioned over and over the sacrifice he and his family were making to provide a decent and moral home for the Tall Tree children.

"We don't really get anything for doing this," he said. "Well, not much, anyway."

When there were breaks in his breathing and noise from his mouth was interrupted, Barbara Borman asked questions. She asked Norman about his art.

"You'll have to show me some of the pictures you've done," she said. "As soon as we get home and all unpacked, you'll have to, okay?"

"Sure," said Norman.

"Yes, ma'am," said Mike Borman. "We use sir and ma'am in our household."

"Yes, ma'am," said Norman, but the conversation was effectively shut down.

"And what about you, Peter?" asked the wife.

"I like to fish."

"Well, we certainly have lots of places to do that. Maybe Mikey…that's our son…maybe Mikey would like to show you some of them."

"That's alright," said Peter. He was looking out the window and avoided moving his eyes to anything inside the car.

"I don't have a fishing pole."

"Your father and I want to ask you about this boy you're seeing."

This was from Nellie Redford's mother. The two women sat at the kitchen table and drank cups of tea. It was a ritual. Nellie would return from school and her mother would put a kettle on to boil while her daughter changed. In the Summer, when school was out, they continued to find themselves at the table each late afternoon right on schedule. Their conversations were typical mother and daughter. Subject matter ranged from extended family developments to fellow parishioners.

"What do you want to know?" asked Nellie.

"He's Indian, isn't he?"

"He is," said Nellie. "But he's also Catholic."

Marjory Redford took this in. Her only child had lived such a sheltered and unthreatened life that discussions of any seriousness were rarely needed. As a junior high school student Nellie had never gone through a boy-crazy time; she had developed late and didn't start her periods until the age of sixteen. Despite the fact that she had grown into a confident and very attractive adult, Marjory Redford's daughter remained, in the eyes of her parents, a girl in need of protection.

"Do you think there might be issues with his race?" she asked Nellie.

"Hell, mother, it's 1969," said Nellie. "Times change."

"Language please," said her mother. "I know they do. I know times change. But we're a little worried that they've not changed enough. Are you worried about how other people might react to seeing you two together?"

"Not one bit," said Nellie as she stood and stepped to

fetch a cookie jar on a counter a few feet away. "I'm not concerned about it one bit."

She took a cookie out and bit a small piece off.

"I love these oatmeal cookies you make. They may well be my favorites."

"We're just wondering how serious all of this is. We're just concerned."

Nellie took a larger bite of her cookie. She spoke while chewing.

"Listen, mom, I don't know how to answer that. I mean, it's not like I've had a bunch of boyfriends. To be honest, Cameron is the first boy…well, the first man that I've not been nervous around. He's just comfortable. And I find him extremely attractive. I know that last part is probably unsettling to you. But I'm not a girl anymore. I don't want you to worry."

Marjory Redford exhaled audibly. She brushed cookie crumbs off the table and on to the floor she would be sweeping shortly. She wanted desperately to ask her daughter if she had had sex with the Indian boy. The Indian man.

But intimacy was not a subject ever discussed in the Redford house. When Nellie went off to college her mother simply assumed that she was a virgin and would remain so until marriage. That her daughter had returned after four years seemingly unchanged from her nervousness and lack of worldly experience was not too terribly concerning. Now there were late nights to contend with. There were questions from people in the grocery store asking about her daughter and the Indian boy.

"They seem to be quite a couple," they would say.

In the end, Marjory Redford did what came most

naturally to her. She skirted the meat of the issue. She left the heavy lifting to God.

"Give me a cookie, Nellie. We're not eating for another two hours."

"My mother tried to have the talk with me."

Nellie and Cameron were eating pie. They sat in their usual booth at the diner in town.

"Father Gillette had the same talk with me. I wonder if they coordinated efforts?" said Cameron. "What'd you tell her?"

"I told her I was comfortable with you. I told her not to worry. I gave her a cookie."

He smiled and placed his hand over hers. As a couple they were not prone to outward displays of affection. They held hands, they occasionally hugged. But for the most part their physical contact was limited to the front seat of Nellie's parents' car. Nellie placed her free hand over his.

"Besides, there's not a lot more to tell her, is there? I could tell that she wanted to ask if we'd had sex. I was kind of glad she didn't. I didn't want to tell her the truth, that we hadn't."

Cameron extricated his hand and ran fingers through his black hair. His effort at a serious face failed as he broke into a grin.

"Are we having this talk now?"

"I love you," she said. "I want to be with you. Listen, I don't want to delve into the past or anything…I mean, I've had a few boyfriends, mostly at college. But I never felt for them what I feel for you. I never wanted to be close to them. Close with them. You know what I'm saying?"

"Yes. I think so," he said. "You need to know that I don't have a lot of experience with what we're talking about. You might be really disappointed."

"I doubt that."

The next Saturday they skipped the movie theater. They did not eat pizza or apple pie. Nellie drove her parents' car to a small town thirty miles away. They had contemplated sneaking into Cameron's room at the back of the church rectory, but that seemed to border on sacrilege. Cameron rented the room as she sat listening to the radio.

The room was vintage northern Michigan. Wood panel walls, artwork of painted forests and deer, carpet so thick you could lose your toes.

He kissed Nellie.

"Can you give me a moment?" she asked.

"Of course."

He went into the tiny bathroom and washed his hands and face. He flipped his hair to one side. He inspected the tiny soaps, the miniature bottle of shampoo. He looked in the mirror.

"Okay," she said from the other side of the door.

She stood naked in the middle of the room. Her arms hung by her sides. For a woman closer to the age of thirty than twenty who could count her sexual experiences on one hand, she was surprisingly comfortable.

Love can often find a way, but lust can always find a way. After a slow and gentle start, after fumbling for a moment with one of the condoms Cameron had brought and after he had entered her, they resorted to the wild. They were connected and pressed together from mouths to feet. They held tightly together hand to hand. They strained to get even closer, body to body. Sweat, saliva, Nellie's wetness, Cameron's semen spurted into the condom's tip.

She placed her head on his chest and lay cupped beside him. Their breathing had calmed. There was no nervousness. They were connected by this.

"I love you, Cameron Tootoo," she said.

"In a lot of tribes what we just did would make us married," he said. "And I love you, too."

And that was enough.

The Tall Trees neither loved nor hated their new home. With the exception of Barbara Borman's greetings in the morning and when the boys returned from school, they were ignored. After an interview with the school's principal, they were placed in the same grades at St. Matthews that they had just finished.

"But, Sister, we just finished those grades at St. Bart's," said Norman.

The heavy-set woman dressed in black held up a pudgy finger. Her face was red and was barely contained by the head piece that girdled her from neck to forehead.

"I believe we have a slightly more demanding curriculum here than at St. Bartholomew's," she said. "And the last thing we want is for you boys to fail."

The decision final, Norman and Peter began a sequence of years that would never change; they were never the brightest boys in class, but they were always the oldest and the biggest. Peter, at least a full year older than the children in his grade, towered over them. The younger of the Tall Tree boys pulled himself back in to his protective cocoon; he spoke only when necessary and he smiled only in the presence of his brother. His grades that first year at St. Matthew's started strong. He'd learned all of that before. By the end of that first year, however, when new subject matter was introduced, he suffered.

The Bormans' son Mikey was twelve. His hair was red and was as long as his father allowed it to get before sending the boy out for a trim. He had a healthy case of acne but didn't seem to care. His table manners were primitive; he burped often during meals.

"Mikey, say excuse me," his mother would say.

"Excuse you," he would respond sending his father into laughter.

The young Borman made clear upon meeting his new house-mates that he had no interest in them.

"Listen, we're not brothers, OK? We're not even blood brothers. Leave me the fuck alone and I'll leave you alone. Stay out of my room or I'm going to kick someone's ass. Got it?"

Mikey played hockey, but poorly. He was boastful about goals he had supposedly scored, but never when the games had been attended by his father. He had a hard time skating backwards. He was loud and used very foul language whenever out of earshot of his parents. He delighted in making fun of Norman each time he came across the Tall Tree boy sketching.

"Art's for girls," he would say. "Boys should play hockey."

"Many of the great artists were boys," said Norman. "Michelangelo, DaVinci. Those guys."

"Who cares?" said Mikey.

On one occasion, as the Tall Tree boys sat at the dining room table, Peter doing homework and Norman sketching,

Mikey breezed through. Clearly an intentional act, he bumped Norman's elbow causing the pencil to scrape across the page.

"Hey," said Norman. "Watch out."

"Sorry. That was an accident," said Mikey Borman.

"Don't do that," said Peter. "That wasn't an accident. I saw what you did. And don't do that again."

"Or what?" said the Borman boy.

Peter pushed away from the table and stood facing Mikey. Although two full years younger than the Borman boy he was taller. Peter had never been in a fight but had a volcanic ocean of fight in him. Mikey was a talker.

"Or I'm going to fight you, that's what. Leave my brother alone."

"I'd like to see you try," said Mikey. The statement was intended to drip with bravado but was delivered with a shaky voice.

Peter returned to his chair and continued his homework on the math problem he had learned a year ago.

The draft notice arrived in late Autumn. Mrs. Baker placed it in front of Cameron as he sat down to dinner with Father Gillette.

"What's this?" he said. "I don't get mail."

After opening and reading the notification that he was to report to a recruiting office in town within 30 days, and that he could expect to ship out to basic training before the end of the year, he took a deep breath. The war was all over the news. Cameron had not taken the time to analyze it. He eavesdropped on more than one phone call between Father Gillette and the parent of a boy being ordered to duty.

The priest was always sympathetic, but always incapable of offering useful suggestions.

"You have to go to Canada," said Nellie Redford when he showed her the notification.

She immediately began to cry. This unsettled Cameron. He had not seen this from the woman he loved.

"No, really," she said as she attempted to wipe the steady flow of tears from her cheeks, "you must go to Canada. Boys are doing it. This war is not right. You can't go away from me and not come back."

She was near shouting. They sat sideways in her parents' car facing each other. Cameron placed his large hands on each side of her face and felt the tears. He was not a complicated man; circumstances such as this were not adroitly dealt with. He had no history dealing with such moments.

"I'm going to go down to the recruitment office and see what they have to say," he said. "There may be a way out. Maybe the Indian thing. But nothing's in cement yet, Nellie. Let's not rush to any conclusions."

"The conclusion is that they're going to send you to war, Cameron. Some war that they can't even tell us why we're in it. The conclusion is that you might go over there and never come back to me. It's not fair. It's not right. I've waited my whole life for you. You can't just disappear."

The entirety of the world that existed between Cameron and Nellie had been pleasant until this moment. The meetings, the falling in love, the sex. It had all been positive. But now, with the woman sitting in this car shouting and crying uncontrollably from fear, with her hands trembling, her eyes swollen, Cameron saw a facet of their relationship that was new. It was serious; it was adult. This new piece of their being together was harsh and blindingly bright. But he did not resent it nor hide from it. This reaction from the woman he loved did not hurt him, it did not give him pause. It showed him his importance. It illustrated the extent to which he was loved. It gave him a sense of wanting to care for her, of easing her pain.

"We'll figure something out, Nellie," he said in as soothing a voice as possible. "Let's don't worry about it until we have to."

She shook her head violently. Her eyes and nose continued to leak.

"I don't want to go home," she said. "Don't you dare think about leaving me, Cameron Tootoo. You're all I have."

Cameron visited the recruiting center the following week. The soldier he spoke with had clearly been stationed at his desk for too long. His hair was cut short; his neck bulged over the too tight collar of his dress shirt. His tie was uneven.

"Cameron, there's not a lot you're going to be able to do. We have lots of Indians in service. Actually, quite a few from around here. Believe it or not, most of them volunteered. You could get a medical waiver, but you look pretty healthy to me. My best advice would be to jump in as quickly as you can. Do your service for your country and get home to the world."

"Have you been there?" asked Cameron.

"Been where?"

"To Viet Nam. Have you been there?"

"I have not. I've been in some hairy shit, but not Nam."

Cameron nodded. Cameron wondered how the hell some fat ass like this could ever safely extricate himself from anything resembling hairy shit.

He also wondered if the Indians the recruiter had mentioned had actually volunteered. It made sense. What were they leaving behind? Discrimination, an uncertain path out from poverty, a very clearly uneven playing field.

The recruiter slid page after page of agreements and instructions across the desk. Cameron scanned each of them and signed on the lines pointed to.

"I've got a bus going to Detroit in three weeks that will take you to basic training. How about we shoot for that?"

Again, Cameron nodded.

"Here's a card with my number on it. If you have any questions, give me a call. You'll get further instructions and guidelines in the mail within a few days. A packet."

Cameron rose to leave. He extended his hand to the recruiter and shook firmly.

"Thanks for your help," he said.

"Thanks for your service to our country," said the heavy-set man.

As he walked through the cold air on his way back to the church Cameron began a mental list of tasks that needed to be accomplished before left. He was unsure how long he would be gone; he was unsure as to whether or not he would ever return. He thought of Nellie and of Mrs. Baker and of the priests. He thought of Sister Collette. And he thought again of Nellie. He pictured he hair, now down to her shoulders. He thought of her blue eyes and of the tiny wrinkles that had begun to appear beside them when she smiled. Her thought of her nakedness and of the way she arched her back when she was on top of him, and he was inside her.

He walked past the entrance to the rectory. It was early afternoon, but the sun had begun its descent. Days were short this far north when the weather was cold. Mrs. Baker would be in her apron. She would be sitting at the large table, probably doing a crossword puzzle, enjoying a little down time before preparing the evening meal for the priests and Cameron.

He stopped at the garden and sat for a few minutes on the bench he had so often shared with Nellie. He loved it that she could be so shy and so engaging at the same time. He loved to hear her laugh. He loved it when she poked fun at him.

He entered the school and climbed the stairs to the second floor to the classroom Nellie and her students occupied. He stood outside the door and peered in through the glass.

There she was. Wearing a dress to the middle of her calf and a blue blouse; she looked as naturally and unaffectedly beautiful as he had ever seen her. He wanted to kiss her. He wanted to take her to the motel out of town and make love with her as forcefully as he ever had. He wanted to taste her and breathe in her scent. He wanted to lie naked with her and listen to her heart beating.

He opened the door and stood in the frame. The children, all in white shirts, stopped and looked at him. Nellie knew where he was coming from, and that he had never set foot in her classroom portended something monumental. She wanted to smile but could not.

After collecting herself, she directed the children to continue with the book they had been reading.

"Silently," she said.

Outside in the hallway, she took Cameron's hand.

"I'm terrified," she said. "I can see it on your face that you have to go."

"I have something I need to tell you," he said. "Don't interrupt."

Nellie released his hand and stepped back one pace. Her breath was trapped in her throat. She perhaps could not have interrupted him had she wanted to.

"I thought about it walking back from the army place. I thought about you and about what it would be like leaving you. I thought about this country, and about what this country has done for me. And the answer to that is 'absolutely fucking nothing.' Then I thought about duty and honor and all of that. I thought about each side of the situation. And I made a decision."

She stood still and looked at the floor. She could feel the beat of her heart in each ear.

"I decided that I want to ask you for a ride to Wawa. I need to see if I can make a connection with anyone who might have known me before I came here. See if I can make a life for myself there. Even if it's just for a while."

She hugged him and ground her body into his. The moment and the emotion were pure. She could not have loved him more than she did in that instant. She didn't even care if one of the nuns saw them holding each other in the hallway. She didn't even think of what her children might be doing.

They kept it to themselves. Cameron was about to break a law. He would be a felon. Not that he was alone in his crime. Hundreds of young men disenchanted with a war they thought unjust had preceded him north of the border. To his understanding, nothing much had been done about it. Whether or not they could ever return to the States was undecided. But in Cameron's mind, Canada wasn't a hell of a lot different from northern Michigan.

"I can come visit you," said Nellie. "It'll be sporadic for a while, but we can still see each other. I mean, it's not that long a drive."

They were lying in bed at the motel. Cameron was on his back; Nellie faced into him and straddled his leg. He could feel the wetness between her legs against his thigh. He said what every man would say in this precise moment.

"I will never stop loving you, Nellie."

He felt it important to talk to the women in his life. After driving the school bus back to the orphanage and watching the children troop into the house, he parked and followed them in. Sister Collette was in her office. She sat at a desk and was writing into a large notebook.

"Hello, Cameron," she said looking up from her book. "How nice to see you. Please come in."

"I'll just take a moment or two, Sister. I have something to share with you."

The nun closed the book on her desk.

"Just making log entries on our children. How they're progressing in school, socially, that kind of stuff. Shall we have a cup of tea?"

"That would be really nice, Sister."

They stepped into the large kitchen and Sister Collette put the kettle on to boil. She collected two mugs from a cabinet and a basket containing a variety of teas and placed them on the table. The mustachioed Mrs. Scumaci was not expected to begin preparations for dinner for another hour. They had the room to themselves.

"Pick one," she said to Cameron and motioned to the basket full of teas.

"I'll have whatever you're having. Thank you."

She took up a box of tea and extracted two bags.

"You want milk or sugar, Cameron?"

"Both, please."

These items placed on the table, Sister Collette brought the steaming mugs, one green, one blue.

"Which one do you prefer?"

He smiled. Her question told him that she had spent her adult life working with children. This would be a question asked of kids. The color of the mugs from which they were about to drink would be important.

"Green, of course."

Now the nun smiled.

"Please tell me your news," she said as she sat across from him.

"Well, there's no easy way to do this so I'll just blurt it out. I've been drafted. They want to send me to Viet Nam."

"Oh, Cameron. I don't know what to say to that. You've been such a fixture here. You've been such a positive role model for our boys. What you did with Peter, the Tall Tree boy, was just remarkable."

He scooped two spoons of sugar into his mug and added a splash of milk from a glass jug.

"I'm not going, Sister. I hope you don't think less of me, but I've given this a lot of thought. I don't know everything about this war, but I know enough to say that it's pointless. It's wrong. I'm not going."

Sister Collette looked straight at him. She sipped her tea.

"It's Irish Breakfast Tea," she said, "do you like it?"

He raised the green mug to his mouth and sipped.

"Very good," he said. "Sister, I'm not a coward. If I felt like it was the right thing to do, I'd be on that bus to Detroit tomorrow."

"What will you do, Cameron? And I know good and well that you're not a coward. We read about this war. We watch the news on television. We see the unrest it is causing all over the country."

"You have to swear not to tell anyone, but I'm going to go home to Canada. To Wawa. I'll just have to try to find a place to live and make a go of it. It's a little frightening to be honest. I've been kind of taken care of for most of my life. But that's my only option. At least as I see it, anyway."

The nun reach across the table with both arms. He put his mug down and allowed his hands to be enclosed between hers. Her skin was sandier and rougher than Nellie's, but her hands held just as much warmth.

"You will do well, Cameron. You have a gentle soul and you have brought light into many lives, including mine. God will certainly watch out for you. And I will keep you in my prayers."

She released his hands and took up her tea. Her smile was soothing.

"Where were you when I lived here?" he said. "Sister

Thecla would have given me a beating for what I just told her."

They hugged on the porch before Cameron returned to his pilot seat on the bus.

"If you can manage it, please write me a note once you're settled," she said.

"Yes, Sister," he replied.

"I want to talk to you about the draft notice I got."

Cameron had entered the warmth and comfort of Mrs. Baker's kitchen. The afternoon was bright. Classical music was playing from a radio plugged in beside the four slice toaster.

She was washing potatoes at the sink, her hands red from the cold water.

"Tell me," she said as she turned to face him.

"I hope you won't think less of me…I know that at least one of your sons was in the Navy for a while…but I can't go. I'm not going. I have a long list of reasons…"

"You don't need to give me any reasons, Cameron," she interrupted. "It's a hard decision. You're a good and strong man. Your reasons are your own."

"You've been as close to a mother to me as anyone in my life. I want you to know how much I appreciate everything you've done for me."

"Where will you go. What are you going to do?"

Cameron laid out the plan. He had enough money saved, just barely, to get a cheap apartment or a room in Wawa. He was unsettled at not knowing the job market, but he was confident that he could turn his hand to just about anything. He had been a gardener and a maintenance man; there were no jobs beneath him.

"When?"

"Soon," he said. "Miss Redford is going to drive me."

"Will she be coming back, or is she staying with you?"

Cameron and Nellie had stopped trying to hide the fact that they were in a relationship. Still, they remained uncomfortable with over-the-top public displays of affection. There were the occasional comments regarding their mixed races that came from unenlightened townsfolk, but these soon began to slide off their skins without notice. They remained circumspect because it was in their nature to do so. Cameron was aware that Mrs. Baker and the others in his circle of life knew about Nellie, he simply did not expect a question about her.

"She's coming back. She has her teaching to do."

"Love will find a way, Cameron. It always does."

"I've heard that," he said. "You need any help with the potatoes?"

Cameron had lived in cramped quarters. As part of his compensation from the church he had been given a small room with an adjoining bathroom. He had saved a good portion of the monthly checks he received. This was not out of frugality as much as an absence of space to put anything he might have purchased. His bank account was slightly north of a thousand dollars, and this bothered him.

It also bothered him that he knew relatively nothing about his destination. He had memories of Wawa. It was on the shores of Lake Superior. The rez was on the outskirts of town and was, at least to his memory, shabby and run down.

He remembered his parents as having been proud of their ancestry. He remembered his mother's smile.

He and Nellie were to leave in three days. The waiting troubled him. He asked her far too often if she had arranged for the use of her parents' car.

"Cameron, they're not going anywhere. They never go anywhere. They'll let me use the car. Relax."

"I could take a bus," he said.

They were sitting in his tiny room at the rectory, having determined that no sins were being committed if their clothes remained on. Nellie sat on the edge of his single bed, Cameron in a chair beside his desk.

"Cameron, don't do this."

"Do what? It's a hell of a long drive all the way to Wawa and back. Maybe I shouldn't put you through this. It's my problem."

"That's the most hurtful thing you've ever said to me. You take that back! How is this not my problem, too? How is it not my problem that the man I love, that the man I've waited for my whole life is about to leave me? Explain that to me, Cameron."

He went to her and sat on the edge of the bed. He put his arm around her. He brushed her hair back.

"I'm sorry, Nellie. I'm worried. I'm headed to the unknown. It's a bit frightening. And…I didn't want to share this with you…but I don't have a lot of money."

"I do," she said smiling. "God, is that all? I was worried it might be something big, that you were leaving me for good, that you were tired of me and that this was your chance to get the hell away."

He laughed.

"I can't take your money, Nellie. I'm leaving you only until we can be together again, but I can't take your money."

In the end, of course, Nellie won the discussion. She pointed out that they were now soul mates, that this separation was merely temporary, that the money would help sustain their relationship while he was gone.

"It'll help get you settled," she said. "It'll help you find a place where I can come and stay over the Summer. Just make sure the bed is bigger than this one."

"I get it," he said in as terse a voice as he had ever used with her. "I'm taking the money because you want me to. But you're getting every penny of it back eventually. Remember that."

She knew that his feelings were hurt a bit and that it genuinely bothered him to have to accept her charity. But she also knew that it was the right thing to do and that his uneasiness would pass.

"If we're going to be living in sin next Summer when I come up there, maybe we should practice a little more," she said as she placed her hand on his lap. "Maybe we should do a little practice sinning right here in your room."

"Technically, it's not really my room anymore. I mean, I told Mrs. Baker that I'm leaving."

He rose and slid his pants and underwear down. Nellie Redford, the fourth grade teacher who lived with her parents, took him in her mouth.

It was three hours to the International Bridge in Sault Ste. Marie. It was a Friday morning, and Nellie had taken a day off. Mrs. Baker had packed sandwiches and cookies in a large brown bag. There was a thermos with hot tea and tiny packets of sugar for Cameron.

On the Canadian side of the bridge, they were asked why they were entering.

"My friend's actually from here. We're seeing some sights."

Assured that the car did not contain firearms or alcohol, the guard waved them through.

The scenery on the drive north to Wawa was Winter postcard material. The lake was frozen over, and drifts of ice and snow rose to meet the coastline as if each wave had been frozen instantly while nearing the shore.

"I bet it's beautiful in the Summer," said Nellie. "I can't wait to come back up."

They pulled into the town of Wawa as the sun was setting. The temperature was well below zero. They checked into a motel and shared the shower before heading out for their dinner.

"That's the first time we've ever been in a motel room and not made love," said Nellie as they drove to the restaurant the motel clerk had suggested.

"The night's young," he said as he slid his hand between her legs.

They ate fried lake perch with boiled potatoes and a salad. As a treat, they each drank two bottles of beer. Back in the room, they fell asleep in each other's arms within seconds of climbing into bed.

The next morning, they saw the sights. They drove through the town and out to the rez. By noon, they had seen just about everything there was to see.

They bought a newspaper and checked the classifieds for places to live. There were few listings for help wanted, but the motel clerk assured them that things would loosen up as the season moved towards Springtime. There was an iron mine; there were farms needing help.

"There's stuff you can do in the meantime," said the woman manning the desk. "My husband and I know everyone in this town. We'll find you something to keep you busy and out of trouble. You got a vehicle?"

"Not yet, but I intend to get one pretty soon. Some beater just to get around."

"Well, we can help with that, too. You really don't need one as small as this town is. As long as you don't mind walking in a little cold weather."

As Nellie and Cameron walked and drove their way around the town, two things caught their attention. The first was that not one person had asked Cameron why he was interested in moving to Wawa. The townspeople had to know that there was an unpopular war consuming the citizens of their neighboring country. They watched the news. The saw the demonstrations. They were aware of the fact that many boys from the states had transplanted to Canada to avoid the draft, but not one time was the question asked of Cameron Tootoo.

They also noticed a difference in attitude in the way they, as a mixed race couple, were treated. More accurately, there was an absence of attitude. There had been only the occasional comment while out on a date in Marquette, but there had always been a hint of disapproval hanging in the air around them. There had been looks; there had been whispers.

But in Wawa none of that was on display. The people with whom they interacted seemed not to care one bit. They noticed this, and they liked it.

On Sunday they went to early mass. The church was simple. It had not the grandeur nor the gravitas of St. Bartholomew's. The stained glass windows were tiny.

After mass they drove to the motel. Nellie had packed her bag and it rested on the bed.

"I don't want to leave," she said.

"It's only for a while," said Cameron.

The held each other in the center of the room. Neither wanted to be the first to let go.

"You need to get going. I don't want you driving in the dark," said Cameron.

He walked her to the car and kissed her cheek as tenderly as he ever had.

"It's only for a while," he said again.

She smiled. Her tears settled into the tiny wrinkles beside her eyes before sliding down her cheeks.

"It's only for a while," she said.

On Peter Tall Tree's fifteenth birthday he gave Mikey Borman a beating. It had been long coming. Mikey had learned to keep his distance from the younger of the Tall Tree boys. He poked fun at Norman whenever Peter was out of earshot, but never when there was a threat of being heard. Peter was six feet tall and had begun to develop the musculature of a grown man. His black hair was shoulder length. His hand-me-down clothing now came from men.

Barbara Borman had baked a chocolate cake. No one

sang Happy Birthday as she carried it to the table after a dinner of hamburgers and oven-baked French fries.

"That looks good," said Mike Borman. "What do you say, Norman?"

"It's Peter's birthday, not mine." Then, to Mrs. Borman: "thank you very much, Mrs. Borman."

"I wonder if Indians celebrated birthdays in the olden days?" said Mikey. "I wonder if they made cakes and had candles?"

"I don't know about the cakes and candles, but of course they celebrated birthdays," said Barbara.

"I wonder what they got for their birthdays. A new tomahawk? A new bow and arrow?"

"Mikey, be nice," said Barbara.

"Maybe when they got older, they got a new peace pipe," said Mr. Borman to his son's delight.

This banter went on throughout desert. When Mrs. Borman had cleared the dishes and disappeared into the kitchen, her husband parked in an easy chair in the living room and turned on the television.

Norman grabbed the bookbag he had left at the front door and returned to the table to do homework. When Mikey went upstairs to his room, Peter followed.

"What do you want? What're you doing in my room?" asked Mikey.

Peter closed the door behind him.

"I just wanted you to know that you're a fucking asshole," said Peter. "Your jokes are stupid. You think we don't know we're Indian? Why does that bother you so much?"

"Get out of my room, you fucking half breed."

"I'm not a half breed, stupid. I'm full blooded. And make me get out of your room."

It wasn't much of a fight. The tiny bit of athletic ability Mikey had been developing on the hockey rink all but disappeared from lack of use when his father became tired of driving him to and from games and practices. He had not skated in a couple of years. Not that he'd of had anything approaching a chance of winning a fight with Peter even if he'd continued on in sports. The years of frustration, as well as the countless jokes at his brother's expense fueled Peter's anger. After Mikey Borman pushed him in the chest Peter hit him precisely five times, all with his right hand, all flush in the mouth.

Peter descended the stairs and took his jacket off the wall hook in the hallway.

"Go check on Mikey," he said to Mr. Borman. "I just hit him."

He opened the front door and walked out of the Borman house for the last time in his life.

What followed, after the police had found Peter walking the streets in the center of town, and after placing him in an empty jail cell, was standard practice. Especially for Indians. Especially in 1975. Two days later Peter was sent by court order to a juvenile facility downstate. Norman was removed from the Borman home and, over the course of the next several years, bounced from one foster home to another. As there existed no one in either boy's life to facilitate a call, the Tall Tree brothers did not speak to each other for three years.

2000

Isabel drove north with a plan of spending a couple days with her parents in Columbus before continuing on to Sault Ste. Marie. Jack Storey was a mid-level accountant at a large firm. He was a steady provider for the family and a conscientious father. Isabel's mother Janie had been a stay-at-home mother through her daughter's young life. Her only personal indulgence was the study of Tai Kwan Do. Twice a week for as many years as she could remember Janie drove to the Columbus YMCA for lessons. She captured her black belt in 1991 and retained an incredible level of flexibility even now, into her fifties.

Members of the Storey family were not given gracefully to physical displays of affection. When Isabel walked through the front door unannounced that Sunday afternoon her father did not get up immediately from the reclining chair he occupied.

"Well, I'll be damned," he said, "hello, Isabel."

She dropped her backpack and walked to him. She bent and gave him a hug that lasted precisely one second.

"Hi, Dad. Don't get up."

"Nonsense," he said rising from the chair.

"Your mother's in the kitchen. I want to see her reaction."

Janie Storey's reaction to seeing her daughter for the first time in over a year was equally muted. She hugged Isabel and motioned to a chair at the table.

"Who wants iced tea?"

"You taking a little time off work?" asked her father.

They were sitting around the table in the brightly-lighted kitchen. Decorative woven baskets hung like pictures on the yellow walls. There was nothing held in place by cute magnets on the refrigerator. Isabel's mother had poured out large tumblers of tea and had placed a bowl filled with pretzels in the center of the table.

"More like a sabbatical," said Isabel. "I decided to leave Kalkan. I'm going to do a little traveling and see where I land."

To her father, a man who had performed basically the same tasks at the same company his entire working life, this was like hearing that his daughter was joining a carnival.

"That sounds exciting," said her mother.

"You just got this big promotion," said Jack. "What happened?"

"I'm not sure, Dad. I do know this…I was doing all the work and was watching the children make all the money. That was frustrating."

"But that's the way it works, Isabel. In a family company that's the way it works."

"There's other stuff involved that I really prefer not to go into. I will say that Mr. Khan is really starting to lose it. It's a matter of time until the kids get control of everything. I just decided to check out before the crap hits the fan. This is really a good time for me to make a move."

"But shouldn't you have secured a new job before leaving the last?"

At this, Janie Storey raised her hands as if saluting Jesus at a tent revival.

"Jack, she's a big girl. I'm sure she's considered all of her options. She knows the right moves to make."

He resigned himself to his wife's way of thinking. He sipped his tea and chewed on a pretzel.

She stayed in Ohio for two days. She attended Tai Kwan Do with her mother Monday afternoon and boiled lobsters for dinner that night.

"For somebody with no income, you can sure splurge with the best of them," her father said.

He sat at the head of the table and wore a giant plastic bib over his short sleave dress shirt and tie. A coating of melted butter made his chin shine.

"I have a few crumbs stored away. Don't worry about me," said Isabel.

She ate breakfast with her parents on Tuesday morning. Intentionally ambiguous, she mentioned that her plan was to drive south, to see some sights, to scope out potential locations and career opportunities. She didn't like it that she had been evasive. She sensed that it bothered her father. His life was ordered; all the numbers were in the right columns in his world.

But she was intent on staying true to the plan. Although extremely unlikely in her mind, the prospect of someone showing up at her parents' door and asking questions about their thief of a daughter had to be considered. If someone were ever to follow her trail, she wanted the trail to end in the driveway of her parents' home in Columbus, Ohio.

The drive north to Lake Superior was longer than she had remembered. It was March and the snow had disappeared from all but shaded areas several yards off the highway. The five mile bridge across the Straits of Mackinaw was exhilarating. She was truly waist-deep in a new adventure now, and this made her brain tingle.

There was a genuine sense of separation that enveloped her as she drove off the bridge and entered the Upper Peninsula. It was real. She was gone. She was now a changed person.

Isabel checked into a different motel than she had used on her previous trip. Her Genesis Engineering credit card was getting a workout on this trip. She had established an automatic payment process with the bank; no monthly statements would need to be mailed anywhere.

She ate fried chicken in her room that first night. She sipped away at two glasses of Chardonnay and attempted to be interested in what was on television. She thought of calling her parents. She thought of calling Arby. For the first time since embarking on this adventure she felt alone.

Paul Sundeen owned and operated a real estate office on the edge of town. He was a short man with a love of cheap bourbon and glazed donuts. The office he rented was furnished with old and damaged chairs and a desk he had picked up along the way at yard sales. He wore suspenders every morning and slicked his hair back with gel.

"You must be a Gordan Gecko fan," said Isabel as she accepted his invitation to sit.

An advertisement poster for the movie *Wall Street* was on one wall. A crocheted sampler stating *Greed is Good* adorned the other.

"It's a lifestyle," said Sundeen. "It's my motivation."

"Well, let's hope you won't have to practice it on me," said Isabel.

Sundeen smiled with as high a level of condescension as she had ever been subject to. Isabel Storey had run an empire. She had been responsible for a quarter of a billion dollars in assets and had ruled over hundreds of employees. She had conducted negotiations with king-makers. All before celebrating her thirtieth birthday. And here she was sitting with this man who had done none of that. Here with this man who, on a good month, rented out one apartment for some lucky customer who entrusted the property to him. If Sundeen were to actually sell a home, laws of physics would unravel. Isabel fought the urge to leave. Maybe the next asshole would be worse.

"I understand from our phone call that you have a place for me to look at?" she said.

"I got a couple, actually. Can I call you Isabel?"

She nodded.

"I got a nice two bedroom house right off the main street. It's been refurbished recently...new appliances, new carpet."

"Price?" she asked.

"It's six fifty a month. Of course, you'd have to put down one month as security. But that's common practice, Isabel."

"Yeah," she said. "I've rented before. What about the other place?"

"It's a little pricier, but still two bedrooms," he said, "eight bills a month, but you get a view of the water."

"Do you have time to show them to me?" she asked.

"I got all the time in the world, sweetie," said Sundeen.

She rose to go and glanced at the crochet work.

"Who made this for you?"

"I did it myself," he said. "Weird, huh? That a man would like to crochet?"

"Not at all," said Isabel. "My last boyfriend was big into needle work."

Sundeen's station wagon wouldn't start, so they took Isabel's car. As she drove the short distances from place to place, Sundeen gave her a brief history of the town through the filter of his own experiences.

"I flipped that place a few years ago. That house over there was used by a drug dealer to sell his stuff."

"What kind of stuff?" she asked.

"Marijuana."

As they headed back to Sundeen's office, she selected the nicer of the two rentals.

"Remember that you'll need to fill out the paperwork in the name of my company," she said.

"Of course," said Sundeen with an all-knowing sneer of a smile. "Remember, Isabel, if you ever want to buy something here, to put down some roots, I can help with that. I have no problem getting into financing for the right clients."

"I'll remember that, Mr. Sundeen. Thank you."

Sitting in the ratty chair back in his office, Isabel glanced at the mounds of paperwork that littered his desk. Sundeen was busy, head down and focused on filling in the paperwork on behalf of Genesis Engineering. She couldn't help but notice the overdraft notice from a local bank that sat on top of one of the large piles. Probably a massive corporate takeover that went bad she thought.

She declined his invitation to lunch. As she drove back towards her motel, she detected a whiff of Sundeen's aftershave. It was sickly sweet and didn't disappear completely for two days. Some sort of chemical compound of engine coolant and bat guano.

She furnished her new home as she had furnished her last apartment. A table and two chairs in the kitchen and dining area, a sofa and one easy chair in the living room, a bed in the larger of the two bedrooms. Pots and pans, dishes and cooking utensils were equally as Spartan.

Never much of a plant person due to her hectic schedule and the demands of traveling for her job, Isabel installed three varieties of indoor ferns. She selected them for ease of care more than any aesthetic quality. On occasion, after downing a few glasses of wine while cooking dinner, she talked to them.

She joined a gym at the college and immediately settled into a routine of working out each morning. Although she was ten years older than almost everyone else utilizing the place, she was clearly one of the fittest. After having missed several days due to her visit with her parents and subsequent drive to Sault Ste. Marie, her workouts were maniacal.

A week into her new life she decided to branch out. A job would mean a paycheck and that would necessitate a bank account. She believed herself to be overboard with caution but was still only a few weeks out from leaving Memphis and Kalkan. She refused to let down her guard.

The next morning, after spending an hour in the gym, Isabel showered and dressed. She went light on the makeup and pulled her hair back in a short ponytail.

The Town of Sault Ste. Marie had become overshadowed by the Chippewa Tribe. When federal and state restrictions governing gambling were eased several years earlier, the tribe had joined Native American communities all over the country in quickly building a casino. The place was modest by big city standards. It housed fifty slot machines, ten blackjack tables, a couple of roulette wheels and a table for dice games. Intended to pay for itself in five years, it did so in one. Tribal leadership had counted on a few locals and a significant percentage of tourists to deposit hard-earned cash into their new endeavor. What they had not counted on was the steady stream of gamblers driving across the bridge from the larger city in Canada. Casino cashiers knew the exchange rates and pushed thousands of dollars a day in multi-colored chips to their neighbors visiting from the north.

With the steady stream of money flowing into the tribe's coffers, the leadership did the right thing. They invested in their community. An addition to the casino came first. Across the country casinos had become a lucrative option for musicians nearing the end of their run at stardom. Bands that had slipped in popularity began re-emerging on this reservation and that. A theater that could seat five hundred would be put to good use.

Next was a school that would accommodate children from kindergarten to graduation. There was nothing wrong with the education provided by the town's school system. The tribal school was a point of pride. It was private. A class dedicated to the tribe's culture and history was required for each student in each grade level. The young man hired as principal was from South Dakota. Walter Rain had a ponytail and had been educated at Yale. He drove a vintage Land Rover and wore extremely nice suits.

Outside of the tribe, there existed very little community development in town. Once a hub for gangsters running illegal liquor across the boarder from Canada, Sault Ste. Marie had slowly diminished in population and in vitality. The Community Development office on Main Street was a remnant of better times. There were days when the woman tasked with manning the desk received no visitors and answered no phone calls.

It was to the tribal school that she sent Isabel that morning.

"They're always looking for volunteers. You'll like it. They have small class sizes, and the school is beautiful."

After a twenty minute chat with the principal, a man Isabel found engaging and very professional and with superlative eye contact, a meeting was set for that afternoon at three. Isabel would be meeting the teacher for whom she would be a volunteer assistant. Ella Crow taught the second grade and had been asking for help.

Everything in Ella Crow's life was big. She was tall and had the body of a nineteen year-old woman who had just spent her first year of college enjoying marijuana and the dining hall. Not necessarily overweight, she carried herself with a straight spine. She had long black hair that she rarely bothered to put up. A quick brush in the morning and it fell openly to the middle of her back. She also drove a truck.

Ella was straightforward and open about her support of Native American rights and the injustices historically perpetrated on her people by the government. There was no topic in this area that she wouldn't discuss; she could argue with just the right balance of logic and bluster. Had she chosen to study the law instead of education, she'd have made a powerful attorney. Ella was also very openly lesbian. Her truck bore a bumper sticker calling for gay rights; tasteful artwork celebrating the female form hung on the walls of her farmhouse.

After Principal Rain escorted Isabel to Ella's classroom and after he had introduced them to each other and left for other duties, the two women sat on tiny chairs and talked. Isabel rendered a condensed version of her last several years. That she had stolen almost two million dollars was omitted, but the sexual harassment and over-all wackiness of dealing with the Khan family made for fun conversation. Ella either listened with a silent and serious face or broke into loud and all-but-uncontrollable laughter; there seemed no middle ground with her responses.

Ella shared with Isabel what it had been like growing up on the rez. She talked openly about being the only girl in school who was attracted to other girls. The hurtful teasings. The giggles and whispers.

"Standard fare for asshole kids, right?" said Ella.

"What's it like now? I don't want to offend anybody, but we seem to be living in a less-than-sophisticated community, don't we?"

"That's a really nice way of putting it. It's no big deal for the women. Women with women always seem to be given a pass by the straight community. It's a bitch on the boys, though. I've seen some truly horrible stuff happen to gay men…tourists just trying to get away up north and have some fun. And they end up hiding in their motel rooms or worse."

"I hate that," said Isabel.

"We should get a beer," said Ella. "I've got to drive Norman home, but I could come right back. What do you think?"

"Who's Norman?" asked Isabel.

"Long story. I'll tell you over a couple of beers. You in?"

Isabel thought of Arby. Not that this brand new friendship was necessarily destined to become a romantic arrangement. But the thought that it might, certainly did not bother her. Ella Crow was very clearly her type.

"I'm in."

The Sundowner Bar was dark and nearly empty when they walked in.

"Find a place where you want to sit and I'll get drinks," said Ella. "Beers OK?"

"Sure," said Isabel.

She took a seat at a table for two in the corner adjacent to a small stage. The drum set and several amps remaining on stage made her think back to Zach Breeze and The Tornados.

"Jesus," she whispered to herself.

Ella joined her with two bottles of beer and a bowl of mixed nuts.

"So, who's Norman?"

"Local guy. He's the janitor at the school and I rent him the apartment over the garage at my place. He rides with me to work and back. Tough life. He and his brother were in and out of foster homes. His brother Peter got into some real trouble a few years ago. He's doing time for almost killing a guy. I'm not easily scared, but that is one seriously frightening man. I've seen him go absolutely blind with rage at the slightest thing. He's a bomb waiting to go off. Anyway, just a typical case of the fucking government not giving a shit about Natives."

"Tell me about your farm," said Isabel.

"Well, it's the bank's farm. They just let me stay on it so long as I make the mortgage payments. Sixty acres that I lease out to a neighbor. He grows hay for his own horses and sells the rest. I get half of that."

"A woman farmer," said Isabel. "I'm impressed."

"I'll have to have you out some afternoon. Show you the sights. Maybe we could cook on the grill."

"Trust me, Ella, I'm not much of a cook. I almost poisoned my last girlfriend…many times."

"I'll take my chances," said Ella.

The women each drank two more beers. The conversation did not stall; the laughter grew louder as stories and anecdotes became less influenced by inhibition. The Sundowner began to fill with regular patrons. The evening sky outside was beginning to darken.

"I should get going," said Ella. "I have a lesson plan to put together. We can go over it in the morning if you want."

"That would be great. I've never really done a lot of stuff with kids. I'm looking forward to this."

Ella walked Isabel to her car. When they hugged quickly

before separating, Isabel was aware that the top of her head barely reached Ella's chin . She'd never been with a woman this tall. She thought of Arby again, but only for an instant.

"You know, I am checking off quite a list of firsts with you," said Isabel.

They were sitting in Ella's kitchen drinking white wine. Sunshine poured in through enormous windows looking out over the hay pasture. It was afternoon, and they had just returned from a long hike.

"What kind of list?" asked Ella.

"Well, you're the first woman I've hung out with who is so tall, for one. And believe it or not, this is the first time I've ever really been on a farm. Some uncle somewhere in Ohio had a farm and my parents took me there once. But I was very young and hardly remember it."

Ella fetched the bottle of wine from the refrigerator and filled both glasses. She placed the bottle on the table and stepped around and behind Isabel. She placed her hands on Isabel's shoulders and gently massaged her.

"Hang with me, Izzy, and you'll have lots of first time experiences."

"I'm not sure you can do that," said Isabel.

Ella pulled her hands back.

"Do what?"

"I'm not sure you can call me that. Call me Izzy. I mean, my grandmother used to call me that and she was the only one who ever did."

Ella bent and kissed her. It was warm and wet and tasted of white wine and passion.

"Your grandmother ever do that for you, Izzy?" she said with a wide smile.

"Well, not nearly so well as you just did."

Isabel spent three days a week working with the children in Ella's classroom. She loved the laughter and the goofiness on display each day. She treated Ella's lesson plans as gospel. She worked with the children through math problems and sentence structure as if running a board meeting.

From the time she was a high school student and first embraced the fact that she was never going to be comfortable as a partner with a man, Isabel had put the thought of ever having children, ever being a mother, in a dark corner. She had grown up an only child with an extremely small extended family around her, and rarely had the opportunity to engage with little ones. The first time she held an infant, when a neighbor woman brought her newborn to the Storey home to show him to Isabel's mother, it was awkward. Isabel, then fourteen, held the tiny boy as if he were a rare and fragile Chinese vase.

The school kids were surrogate children. Isabel knew that and accepted it. She wondered if that was the reason, consciously or not, that Ella had gone into teaching.

"Izzy, you ever been with a man?" Ella asked her at lunch.

They sat across the child size picnic table in the play area. The children were in the cafeteria eating hamburgers made from some kind of supplement grain with a small representation of beef.

"Like sexually, or just like dating?" asked Isabel.

"Either."

"I dated a couple of guys. One in high school. A jock. Another guy in college who actually turned out to like boys. We made out, but I never had sex with either of them. You?"

"I fucked a couple boys in high school. It was what I thought was expected of me. Failed experimentation."

"I love having sex with you," said Isabel. "You take me over a cliff every time."

It was a Friday and they had made plans to spend the weekend on Ella's farm hiking and watching old movies.

"I'll grab some wine after I get my stuff and water the plants," said Isabel.

"Oh, hi, Norman," said Ella looking beyond Isabel's shoulder.

Isabel turned and waved to the janitor who approached their table.

"Norman, have you been introduced to Isabel? Isabel Storey is our newest teaching volunteer. She works with me."

Norman Tall Tree wore the matching drab green slacks and shirt associated with men who worked with their hands. He was not tall, but he carried himself as a tall man might. His face was lined with years of wrinkles, not so much from smiling as from squinting into the sun. Though he had just celebrated his forty-second birthday, he looked at least a decade older.

He extended his hand and grasped, not firmly, Isabel's.

"It's very nice to meet you," he said. "I've seen you at Ella's a few times...I live above the garage... but I didn't want to invade your privacy."

"Not at all," said Isabel. "That would never be an intrusion. It's very nice to meet you, Norman."

"What's up, Norman?" asked Ella.

"I was just wondering if you were going to need your truck tonight. If I might be able to borrow it for a little. Just to drive into town."

"Got a hot date?" asked Ella.

Norman smiled. His pronounced chin jutted forward.

"Really?" said Ella. "I was kidding. You have a date, Norman?"

"Not a date really. Well, sort of a date. It's with Martha from the cafeteria. We thought we might go to a movie."

"Martha? The girl who works in the back? She's kind of young, isn't she?"

"I'm not marrying her," he said. "At least not yet."

"Sure, you can use the truck. Izzy's coming out for the weekend. If I need to go anywhere, she can drive me. Right, Iz?"

"Thank you," he said. "Back to work."

He departed as quietly as he had arrived. There were trash bins to empty and hallways to mop.

"That's a sad story, but a repeating theme with my people," said Ella. "Kids of other races in America get orphaned, there are safety nets for them. People who have a genuine interest in their well-being. Not with us. We're fucking Indians. We shouldn't be around anymore anyway."

"I don't know," said Isabel. "I lived in Memphis for a few years. Black kids there don't get treated any better. At least not that I could tell. There were haves and have nots, you know? At least here there's the tribe involved. Nice school and all of that."

Isabel wanted to add that the underprivileged kids she was talking about did not have access to money made by legal gambling. They owned no casinos.

"I don't give a shit about black kids," said Ella. "I work towards righting the wrongs my people have had to deal with for centuries. I don't have time for them. They can fight their own battles."

The following Saturday afternoon Isabel and Ella changed from bedclothes...sweatpants and tee shirts... into jeans and sweaters. They laced up their hiking boots and headed out across the hay pasture. Their path was to skirt the edge of the neighbor's farm and climb the gradual two-mile hill that was off to the north. There was a rock outcropping there with a nice view.

A few hundred yards into the hike, they heard voices coming from a loudspeaker of sorts. It was coming from the farm owned by Ella's neighbor. The sound came to them as would an echo coming out of a deep cave. As they walked nearer and nearer, the audio became less garbled.

"It's time for Americans to be Americans again. I'm tired of taking care of all the other races in our country. The blacks, the Indians, the fucking Mexicans. Why do white people have to work as hard as we do just to give them all a handout? We need to take back our country!"

This was followed by applause and cheering. Isabel and Ella were not close enough to see the man who had spoken these words nor the crowd who cheered them. But the speech was followed by a scratchy recording of The National Anthem.

"What the fuck was that all about?" asked Isabel.

They had continued on their hike around the neighbor's farm and begun climbing the slope up to the rocks.

"They're white supremacists. I'm entertained with this

racist bullshit twice a year or so when all these fucking bigots gather at Hostettler's farm. He's big into all that shit. He and I don't speak."

"No doubt," said Isabel.

"He and his mousy wife...you never see her out anywhere without him...are part of this church in town. Son of God something or other. They're over the top with anti-gay, anti-mixed marriage, pro-life shit. If you believe what you hear, they're a pipe-line for babies to be adopted by couples down state. Especially Native babies. Everybody wants one, you know?"

"Sounds like we'd get along famously," said Isabel.

"You'll love this," Ella said, "he has one of those bumper stickers on his truck that says God created Adam and Eve, not Adam and Steve.'"

"I wouldn't have thought Michigan would be the kind of place where these right wing bible thumpers lived."

"We're a hotbed for this shit. Those guys who blew up that building in Oklahoma City, they were from here. There are these militia groups all over the state. Except probably in Ann Arbor."

Norman pulled Ella's truck into the driveway as the two women were returning from their hike.

"Not a scratch, and I filled the gas tank," he said as he flipped her the set of keys.

"How was the date?" asked Ella.

"We had fun. Saw a movie. I don't want you to think that anything happened just because I slept over. We had a few beers, and nobody handles drinking worse than me. Well, my brother."

"I'm glad you had fun," said Ella. "We're going to watch a movie or something. You want to come in?"

"No thanks."

Ella and Isabel passed on the movie in favor of thirty minutes of frenzied sex.

"God damn, Ella, if you make that any more intense, you're going to put me in the hospital. I saw stars."

After showers, they moved to the kitchen and poured glasses of wine. They sat with dripping hair at Ella's table as the sky outside began to move through the rainbow toward indigo. They wore bathrobes and their feet were bare.

"You ever been in love, Iz?"

"Why is it always you who starts these conversations? I feel like I'm a guest on a talk show sometimes. And, yes, I've been in love."

"Tell me about it. What made it real? What made it special?"

Isabel sipped at her wine. She ran her hands through her wet hair. She looked at Ella with eyes as blue as the ocean.

"She stood behind me. There was nothing special. No bells or whistles. No music. She just stood behind me and I knew she was there. If I committed a big crime, if I killed somebody, she wouldn't have flinched. She'd have accepted me for who I was. That's special, right?"

Ella leaned in and kissed Isabel. Just a brush across her lips.

"What happened?" she asked. "Why did it end?"

"I did something stupid," said Isabel. "You know, I've always been one of those girls who, once I start something, I can't leave it unfinished. I mean, I made a good career out of that. I climbed the ladder really fast in a world where women don't get to play too often. So, I started something and finished it. And she couldn't be a part of that."

"And then you came here."

Isabel nodded.

"Then I came here."

"Are you staying? See, I kind of want to know before I go falling off the deep end for you. I mean, if you just want to play around, just keep everything simple, I'm good with that. I'm just wondering if or when you're going to get tired or bored of this place. I'm wondering if you miss the excitement of being an executive and all of that. The challenge."

Now Isabel leaned in.

"I don't know," she whispered. "I truly don't. But I am loving the time we spend together. Can I just leave it at that for a while?"

As Isabel drove home the following morning, she ran the weekend through her head. The hikes that she breezed through as Ella stopped every few hundred yards to catch her breath, the sex, kissing Ella as they showered together, the racist rally at Hostettler's farm, the lasagna Ella made for her, more sex, bottles of wine. And not once, not for an instant during the entire weekend did she stop and worry about work. There were no employee issues to distract her. No payroll to process. No pending profit and loss statement to have to be prepared to discuss. This had been her life for years. She wondered as she drove back towards her rented house in town if she really missed it or just anticipated doing so.

"Let's go to a concert. Want to?"

This was Ella talking to her volunteer assistant while the children were running around the playground over recess. There were only days until Summer vacation, and the volume of the high-pitched squeals heard from the outside had been slowly ratcheting up.

"Sure," said Isabel. "What concert?"

"It's part of a celebration for the Native American community. It's being held at the casino."

"That seems appropriate," said Isabel. "Who's playing?"

"Well, there's a bunch of stuff that happens during the day, it's in two Saturdays. Ceremonial dances, drum stuff, arts and crafts displays. And then the concert starts about four. It's Women With No Feet."

"What?" asked Isabel. "Women With No Feet? I never heard of them."

"That's because you live in a sheltered, executive, suit wearing world, Izzy. They're huge in the lesbian community. They opened for Melissa Etheridge and K.D. Lange, for fuck sakes."

"They must be good. I'm in."

Isabel looked forward to the day of the concert. With school now out for the Summer, there were three extra days to fill. She could only spend so much time in the gym. She enjoyed walking through town and cataloguing the tourists who were now streaming in, but that didn't fill her days. She thought of writing a book, but with the exception of the crime she had committed there seemed nothing in her treasure chest of experiences that seemed of potential interest to anyone but herself.

Ella stayed with her in the rented house the Friday before the big day so that her truck would be available to Norman if needed. Isabel cooked, which was a rarity.

"It's good, Izzy," said Ella as she chewed a piece of marginally over-cooked pot roast.

"I warned you that I'm not a good cook. You don't have to lie to me."

The following morning, they headed out to the rez in Isabel's car. It was approaching eleven in the morning as they were directed by an Indian boy wearing a bright yellow vest to a parking spot nearly a mile from the field adjacent to the casino.

"Wow. I didn't expect this big a turnout," said Isabel.

"We're bigtime now," said Ella. "Indians are in vogue. Everybody wants to be one," she said, "until it's time to really be one, that is."

The open field beside the casino was active. Several large tepees had been erected, and white smoke wafted out of the tops of each. Stalls had been set up throughout the grounds. Demonstrations from blanket weaving to weapons assembly were prominent. In the center of the field, ten men sat in a circle pounding their drums and chanting in rhythm.

Ella seemed to know everyone. As the two women walked from one edge of the field to the other, she was stopped repeatedly with hugs and handshakes from men and women. Isabel took note that, although she was not the only non-Native in attendance, she was very clearly one of just a few. She liked this. She greeted the people Ella introduced her to with firm handshakes and just a hint of deference.

They ate smoked fish for lunch at one of the food stands.

"What kind of fish is this?" asked Isabel.

"This is trout," said the man serving them. He was old as dust and had very fine, white hair down to his shoulders. His face was as wrinkled as a dried apricot.

"It's delicious," she said to him.

"Here," he said, "try some whitefish. Lots of people prefer this to trout."

Isabel took the flaked-off piece of fish from the old man's hand.

"It's good," she said, "but I like the trout better."

"Me too," said the old man.

They bumped into Norman and his friend Martha at an archery demonstration. She was slight as the wind and held his hand as if on a spacewalk. Martha had the high cheek bones associated with being a Native, but her skin color was lighter. Her brown eyes were averted as she was introduced.

"Martha, we've heard a lot about you," said Ella towering over the smallish woman.

"Thank you," said Martha sheepishly.

Isabel took pains not to crush her hand when it was finally extended.

"Have fun, you two," said Ella more as a directive than a suggestion.

"Thanks for letting me use the truck," said Norman. "Hey, Ella, can I ask you something?"

"Sure thing."

Norman extricated his hand from his companion's and motioned for Ella to join him a few steps away.

"We'll just be a second," he said to his date.

Once out of earshot of the others, Norman put his hand to his mouth and spoke through his fingers.

"Would it be alright if Martha came back to the apartment with me? I mean if you don't think it's a good idea, that's fine. We just thought…"

"Of course, it's fine," Ella interrupted. "Hell, Norman, we're all big boys and girls here. You see how often Izzy's out there."

"OK. Thanks."

When Norman had reconnected with Martha's hand and the two of them had moved on to the next exhibit, Ella looked at Isabel and shook her head.

"The man is in his forties, and he acts like a teenager. He asked for my permission to bring his girlfriend to his apartment. This is what society can do to these people. My people. It robs them of their dignity. It crushes their spirits."

"I was more interested in her," said Isabel. "Jeez, I don't know if I've ever seen anyone so lacking in confidence."

"There again," said Ella, "the world my people have been forced to live in is not one that gives a shit about them. God knows what kind of abuses that poor woman has had to deal with."

After visiting a few more exhibits, Isabel jumped at the suggestion to go home and shower before returning later in the afternoon for the Women With No Feet concert. The day was unseasonably warm, and her underarms felt sticky. She'd also had had just about the right amount of hearing how unfairly Native Americans were treated. Of this fact she had no doubt. The constant reinforcement coming from the tall woman she was about to shower with, however, could grow old.

She'd never been in a casino. Even at three in the

afternoon as Isabel and Ella walked through the main hallway, there was a steady supply of noise.

"I never would have thought this place would be this busy at this time of day," she said to Ella.

"This place goes day and night. I think they might stay open until three in the morning on the weekends. Shift workers from Canada. This place makes so much money."

"Is it regulated? Is it taxed?"

Isabel wanted those questions back in her mouth the instant she uttered them. This could lead to a new oratory of Native Americans having to live under the thumb of whites. Ella seemed incapable of passing these opportunities up.

"Of course, it is," said Ella. "That's why the tribe invests so much into all this stuff around us. If it went to the government, we'd never see a penny come back."

Isabel was glad when they had bought large beers and had taken their seats in the auditorium. She leaned over and kissed Ella on the neck. She loved many things about this tall and fierce woman. The minor irritation of hanging out with such a crusader was not that big a deal.

The stage was set up with multiple amps and mic stands. It had the promise of being a loud night. Surprisingly, the opening act was a gray haired man playing an acoustic guitar and singing jazz and folk influenced songs. His music was tepidly received by the crowd, but Isabel liked it.

We had us some good times
We sure liked to dance
The lump in your throat
Matched the lump in my pants

We had us some moments
Deep and profound
But you can find my intentions
In the lost and found

These were the last moments of calm before the main act took the stage. The loudest ovation he received was when the band's lead singer informed the crowd that the opening act had actually been her father. He was already off stage when the polite applause reached him.

The place was filled with women of all ages. The few men sprinkled throughout the crowd seemed out of place.

Women With No Feet, Ella had explained to Isabel earlier in the day, was a band of women, for women. They produced all of their own music; they played all of their own instruments. The only men ever on stage were the roadies who lugged amps and other band equipment to and from the big RV in which they toured.

Their songs were anthems. *Come Munch On My Carpet. I'm Glad You're Not A Boy. I Don't Need No Ugly Cock.* These were just a few. The music was loud, and the crowd was enthusiastic.

"I wonder how many of these women here tonight are going to have sex later?" asked Ella as they filed out of the auditorium.

"I'm guessing I know for sure that two are," said Isabel.

They decided on an early dinner at one of the casino restaurants. They enjoyed a bottle of champagne with crab legs and potato cakes. As they shared a huge slice fudge-covered chocolate cake, their waiter delivered two fruity drinks with tiny umbrellas to their table.

"They're from the man at the bar. The guy with the lavender sports coat."

"I don't know him," said Ella as she glanced over.

"Fuck me," said Isabel. "That's the guy who rented me my house. You know, Gordon Gecko."

Isabel raised one of the drinks in acknowledgement to Paul Sundeen.

"God, I hope he doesn't come over," she said.

"Too bad," said Ella. "Here he comes."

Sundeen's aftershave arrived a split second before he did.

"Good evening, ladies. Isabel, it's awfully nice to see you."

"Thanks," she responded. "And thanks for the drinks. What are they?"

"Tutti Fruities. I invented them myself when I was island hopping in the Caribbean."

"I'm sure they're delicious," said Isabel. "Thanks again."

She turned to Ella in an effort to discontinue the conversation, but Paul Sundeen was oblivious.

"So, did you ladies take in the big concert?"

Ella took another forkful of cake. Isabel place her fork on the table and turned to Sundeen.

"Paul, as you can probably see, we are on a date here. Thank you for the drinks...that was very thoughtful, but please afford us the courtesy to enjoy our evening without interruptions. If there is ever anything I need related to real estate, I'll call on you."

Sundeen looked at Ella and then back at Isabel.

"For sure," he said. "That would be great. Sorry to intrude."

"Not at all," said Isabel icily as she turned back to Ella.

Chastened, Sundeen went back to his stool at the bar. He had never been to the Caribbean, but he had been rejected by attractive women too many times to count. His resiliency was based on distortion of fact; his reality was that women saw him as a successful and dangerous man. The lavender jacket spoke to them.

"See those two babes over there, the ones you brought the drinks to?" he said to the bartender as he reclaimed his seat.

"Sure," said the bartender.

"I'm about a cunt hair away from talking them into a threesome later."

Sundeen smiled as if he had just taken a sip of motor oil.

Norman Tall Tree had never had a relationship with a woman that lasted more than a couple of months. Although significantly less eye-catching than his taller and more muscular younger brother Peter, Norman was not an unattractive man. Quite simply, he lacked anything close to resembling confidence. His teenage years, the span of time which should have provided him with opportunities to grow and develop into a man, had been deprived him. Once his little brother and protector began his own trail from Juvenile Detention to prison, once Norman was on his own and was forced to spend his energies on being invisible to bullies, any development of social skills and confidence was shut down. The boy who had been a good reader and in possession of pronounced artistic ability began to pull inward. Eye contact was rare. He thought of his mother and his brother less and less often.

It came as no surprise when Martha informed him that she wanted to stop dating.

"You've been really nice, Norman. And you have been really fun," she said as he dropped her at the small house she occupied alone. The place had been left to her by the grandmother who had raised her. Martha's mother had moved to Alaska with a seasonal fisherman when she was ten and had not been heard from in years.

"I can't explain it. I just don't want to date anymore."

A thoughtful man with any semblance of relationship history upon which to call might have asked why. But that man was not this man.

"OK, Martha. I'll see you around the school in the Fall."

As he drove Ella Crow's truck back toward his apartment above the garage, he couldn't help but to think of Martha naked. Her body was small. Her breasts, her hands, her feet. She had been only the third woman in his life with whom he had had sex. From what he had believed, she had enjoyed it as much as he did. He cried that night, but only the once. If he allowed himself to feel sorry for spending the majority of his life alone, it could lead to dark clouds.

Norman worked Summers at the famous Soo Locks, the waterways that deliver giant freighters safely from Lake Superior to Lake Huron thirty or so feet below. He performed maintenance on anything needing fixing; he emptied trash cans and cleaned public restrooms. He wore the same drab green clothing as he did at the school. He preferred working with the children to cleaning up after strangers, but the anonymity associated with this job was settling to him.

It came from nowhere.

"Hey, shithead. This garbage can is full."

Norman did not have a phone at his apartment at Ella Crow's. Nor had he joined the millions of Americans who simply could not carry on with their lives without a cell phone. The result was that over the course of the last five years and change, while his younger brother had been incarcerated at the state penitentiary in Jackson, Michigan for assaulting a man while attempting to rob him, they had not spoken. Norman wrote with news of his life, but not often.

Peter's voice carried DNA with it. At its essence, it was incapable of changing from what it had been. Though deeper and sprinkled with the gravel that comes from age, it was the boy's voice that Norman knew instantly.

He stood tall and straight in a new pair of jeans, a new button-down dress shirt and new laced shoes. His hair was long and fell freely down his back. His chest was larger than Norman remembered, and his arms, even covered by the white shirt, were like the trunks of small trees. His left eyebrow was cut in half by a scar.

The men did not embrace or even shake hands.

"When did you get out?" asked Norman.

"Yesterday. They give you one set of new clothes and a couple hundred bucks. I set up my parole officer for here, so I hopped on a bus last night."

"How did you know I'd be here?"

"I didn't. You mentioned working here in a letter last Summer. I just gave it a shot."

"It's good to see you, Peter. It's good to see you out of there."

"Would it be alright to crash with you for a bit, just until I get my shit together a little?"

"I'll have to ask Ella. She's my landlady. But I'm pretty sure she won't mind. She's a member of the tribe and is always going on about how we need to support other Natives, you know?"

"What time do you get off?"

"I get off at three, but I rode my bike to work today. I don't have a car and I don't like bugging Ella for rides if I can help it."

"How far to your place?" asked Peter.

"A little over five miles."

"I could walk that."

"Let's do this," said Norman, "I'll ride home and talk to Ella about you staying with me for a while, and then I'll borrow her truck and come back and get you. How about I meet you back here at five?"

"That sounds good. I'll see you at five."

"I'm glad you're out, Peter. That must have been bad for you."

"You get used to it. If you follow all the rules, it's not so bad."

"You need any money right now?" asked Norman.

"I'm good," said Peter. "Hey, Norman, are you still drawing? Do you still do your art?"

"I haven't in a while, but I'm thinking about it."

Norman was relatively certain that Ella would not object to having his brother stay with him for a bit. As he rode his aging bicycle out of town and toward Ella's farm that afternoon, he developed a game plan that would help his brother break the cycle of small time crime and big time violence. He would ask someone at the tribe to find him a job. So long as Ella didn't object, he would let Peter sleep on his sofa. He would cook for him and would keep him away from bad influences. He would keep him away from alcohol. He would, truly for the first time in their lives, look out for and protect his little brother.

"Of course, it's alright," said Ella. "I mean, I don't want it to be permanent, but for a while, until he gets his feet on the ground, of course."

"Once he and I both have jobs, I think we'll buy a car. I hate asking you, but…"

"Here," she said as she flipped him her set of keys.

The tribe found Peter a job at a garage. He had taken a few classes in prison and understood the basics of car repair. With both brothers working, it took less than eight weeks for them to salt away sufficient cash for a down payment on a car. It was a ten year-old, four door behemoth of a Cadillac. Its dull red exterior was sprinkled with bondo patchwork. It was the first time in their collective lives that either of the Tall Trees owned a vehicle.

"I can take care of this car," said Peter. "I can make this run forever."

The brothers decided to find a larger place and move in together. The five miles into and then back from town each day was an inconvenience, especially with one vehicle. Norman told Ella a couple weeks before they were scheduled to return to school.

"I hope that this isn't a pain for you, Ella. You've been like a family member to me."

"We're from the same tribe, Norman. We are family. You've been a great tenant, but a better friend."

A week later Ella loaned the men her truck. It took only two trips to the dilapidated two-story house in town that they had rented. It was, all things considered, a dump, but it was their dump. The floorboards creaked under ages-old carpeting, and it would be a bitch to heat in the Winter, but it was home.

The first day of school was exciting for Norman. He had not worked at the locks for the two weeks preceding the return to school, and he had enjoyed cleaning and fixing up their rented house.

That morning he dropped Peter off at the garage and drove to the rez.

"I'll pick you up at five," he said to his brother.

Norman entered the building and inspected the items in the maintenance closet. Mop and bucket, broom and dustpan, a shelf-full of a variety of cleaning products. He walked though the building and inspected each classroom, then the bathrooms. All was in order. His empire was intact.

He walked through the cafeteria and back into the kitchen where, later in the morning, he expected to see Martha working away preparing lunch for the children. She would be wearing the hair net he often made fun of. His stomach was nervous at the thought of seeing her.

But it was not to be avoided. He knew that she would be there, and he knew that she would be expecting to see him. This is the kind of awkwardness that comes attached to workplace romance.

A few minutes before noon, when he knew the children would be lining up in the hallway to begin their slow and steady march to lunch, he entered the kitchen. He carried a broom as if armed for battle.

Her hair was a bit longer, and she was very clearly pregnant. Her eyes connected with his, but only for an instant. Her mouth attempted to form words but could not. He felt blood rising to his temples and to the back of his eyes. The air was instantly warm and made the room spin.

"I wanted to talk to you, to tell you why I didn't want to date you anymore," she said. "But I'm just in this...I don't know what to say. I was just in this bad place. I didn't know what else to do."

They were sitting at a tiny picnic table in the playground. Lunch had been served. The children were back at their desks.

"Is this baby mine?" asked Norman as he stared at her feet.

"It's embarrassing," she said. "I don't know. There was one other person, right before you. I never did anything with him after you and I started going out. I promise and hope to die."

"What are you going to do?"

"Adoption. I'm putting it up for adoption. There's this church, they find people...like, really good people who can't have their own babies. They take care of everything. They pay all the medical costs and all the other stuff."

Norman was silent. He had never really had parents, and now the thought of possibly being one was overwhelming.

He had settled into a practical life with Peter and reveled in the role he now played in keeping his brother out of trouble. If this baby were his, well that was too much to think about just now.

"Do you want to keep this baby, Martha? I could help you with that. Peter could help."

Martha had never been quick to grasp anything. The grandmother who raised her reminded her of this constantly.

"Make your decisions slow, girl. Your brain don't work too fast. It's who you are."

Martha looked up at Norman. He remained focused on her feet.

"What if it's not yours?" she asked.

"Then we'll pretend it's mine."

She began to cry. These tears had been forming for weeks as she dreaded this conversation. Had she been able to find a different job so as to avoid this talk, she would have taken it. But she had a house to keep, a mortgage payment to make.

"I already took the money," she said. "It's too late."

Zach Breeze booked the Blue Sky Studio in Nashville for a month. There were studios in Memphis that were every bit as cutting edge and modern as Blue Sky; he wanted to be away from his day-to-day as a step towards total immersion into his music. He also looked forward to not having to remind anyone that his name was not Buster. And he wanted to wear boots. The Tornado drummer, a modestly talented musician who lived with his mother and worked the overnight shift as a desk clerk at a hotel, was able to make the trip. The other Tornados were replaced with four studio musicians arranged for by the owner of Blue Sky. It was big time. Zach and the lone Tornado had never been around anyone who could play like the three men who had joined them. They learned Zach's songs after one playing; they were tight.

The whole studio experience came with a price tag of just over fifty thousand. Zach had convinced his father that it was a sound investment.

"If we sell ten thousand records, you'll have your money back. Everything over that is gravy."

"Is this a business we're investing in, Buster? Is there any property that comes with it?"

Along with every other person who had come into contact of any kind with Khalid Khan over the past few months, Buster was painfully aware that the old man's faculties had begun to rapidly desert him.

"Kind of," said Zach. "We own the property that will be the record. The rights to the property kind of thing. If it sells a million…well, we'll be bringing in some very serious cash."

This obfuscation was probably not necessary; Khan spent more than this on new cars every year for Buster and Allie. But it sealed the deal and sent Zach on his way to country music stardom.

"That's excellent work, Buster," said the old man. "Send in Roberta with my personal checkbook."

Zach reserved two rooms at the Emperor House Hotel in Nashville. The drummer had never stayed anywhere approaching the poshness of the Emperor. He began loading the tiny soaps and plastic bottles of shampoo and body lotion into his suitcase the first night they were there. If the housekeeping ladies replenished the supply each day, he was sure he'd be set for months when he got home to his mom's place in Memphis.

The goal was to record and polish up one track every other day. The ten original songs Zach wanted to be included on this first album were all potential hits. With the help of the studio guys, as well as some serious promotional investment he was sure he could talk his father into, Zach was confident that he was on his way.

He invited the studio guys to the Emperor for dinner after the fifth day of recording. Two of them accepted; the bass player and the guy who played rhythm guitar had other plans.

"I've never been around anyone who can play like you guys," said Zach's Tornado drummer.

"Thank you, Eddie," said Bob, one of the guitar players the studio had provided. "We like playing with you. I like your songs a lot, Zach."

"I'm not the player you guys are," said Zach. "If I'm going to make it in this business, it's going to be as singer songwriter."

"For sure," said Bob.

After Zach had signed the check for dinner to his room, the studio guys thanked him and went outside. They had driven together and now waited for the valet to bring the car around. Bob lit a cigarette.

"You gonna play on Zach's next album?" he asked. "You know, after this one goes platinum?"

The other man chuckled.

"Jesus Christ, have you ever heard such shit?" he asked. "The girl done nabbed my heart, or whatever the fuck that line was. It's too bad our names have to go on the fucking album. What an embarrassment. Dinner was good, though."

The valet brought the car around and the two studio guys got in and drove off. They were oblivious to the fact that Zach Breeze, the guy who was paying union scale dollars for their time, had followed them out of the hotel. It was not Zach's intention to eavesdrop; he had simply wanted some air before going back to his room to watch videos on Country Music Television. But he had heard every word.

The news that his only son had killed himself in a Nashville hotel all but completely severed the connections running from reality to Khalil Khan's brain. Had he wanted to overcome this tragedy, he probably could not have. Buster's death pushed him to the precipice. Once Khan was swallowed by the black hole of dementia that had slowly been exerting its gravitational force on him, he gave up. He didn't fight it. He didn't whimper.

Allie knew something had to be done. Each morning after her brother's death she visited the old man's office, and each morning it was the same. Her father sat behind his huge desk. His eyes focused on nothing. He wore mix and match sets of pajama tops and bottoms, dress shirts and slacks; sometimes, he wore nothing at all.

Through all of this Roberta Bertolli was a saint. She showed up to what had quickly become a meaningless job every day, and often on Saturdays simply to help Allie out. She helped the owner's daughter dress the old man. She even helped Allie shave him when absolutely necessary.

"I know I have to do something," said Allie. "He needs around the clock care. This isn't sustainable."

With the help of a visit from social services, Allie arranged for her father to be placed in a full-service nursing home. Khalil was dressed in a version of his normal uniform; he looked almost normal in a baby blue suit and tie. Allie had selected the yellow socks which seemed to please him.

That afternoon, after the old man had been safely ensconced in his new home, after Allie and Roberta had made the drive to Khan's home in the hills and grabbed up clothing and personal items to be delivered the next day, they sat in his office.

"Tough day," said Roberta. "I know this day had to be awful for you, Allie. But, my God, you handled it well."

"I just feel bad for daddy. He worked so hard for all of us. It breaks my heart to see him like this."

"We don't know," said Roberta. "This might be the most at peace he's been in a long time…maybe ever."

"I'm overwhelmed," said Allie. "I've been praying for strength, but I don't know if I have enough. I have to meet with the lawyers, with the banks. I still have to do something about Buster's stuff…his house, his belongings. It just hit me, Roberta, that I'm all that's left. For the whole company and everything else. I'm all that's left."

Allie put her head in her folded arms on Khan's desk. Her shoulders raised and fell as she sobbed openly. Roberta stepped behind her and put her hands on her shoulders.

"It will be alright, Allie. You're stronger than you think you are."

After the delivery trip to the nursing home the following morning, Allie and Roberta drove to the office of Khan's personal attorney, a white-haired southern gentleman named

Rufus Sapp. Sapp had known Khan for decades and had been a voice of moderation when Khalil had threatened to sue just about every person with whom he ever did business. He knew Buster and Allie from years of his firm's holiday soirees that Khan and his children were always invited to.

"Come in, young lady," he said softly as he took Allie's hands in his own. "Such a terrible ordeal you are going through. I am here to help you, Allie. You can be certain of that."

"Thank you, Mr. Sapp. Thank you."

"Mr. Sapp, I'm Roberta Bertolli, Mr. Khan's personal secretary. We spoke on the phone."

"Welcome, Ms. Bertolli. Please, have a seat."

They were seated at the large and elegant table in Sapp's board room. Portraits of hunting dogs poised for action hung on every wall. Sapp had placed a file folder in front of his chair.

"Coffee or tea for either of you?" he asked.

When the women had declined his offer, and when he had opened the file folder with surprisingly few pieces of paper in it, he presented the options to Allie.

"Everything is owned entirely by your father," he told her. "As all of these companies are privately held, he controls one hundred percent of the stock. I need to ask you, Allie, what would be your intentions relative to the continued operation of KalKan?"

"What? Are you asking me if I want to continue to run it without my father? How could I do that? Gosh, I wouldn't know where to begin to know how to do that."

"Well, we need to think about that. An unfortunate reality is that your father cannot be burdened with decisions of any kind. We will need to take steps to have him declared not of sound mind. This is necessary for any number of reasons, first and foremost among them is the perpetuation of the company's wealth."

"I'm not sure I know what any of that means, Mr. Sapp."

"Please, both of you, call me Rufus. We're going to be spending a good deal of time together for the next several weeks. Familiarity is essential."

"Rufus," said Roberta, "are you saying that we…that Allie needs to have her father declared incapable to running the company? That his duties and responsibilities will fall to her?"

"Yes, Roberta. These steps are not mandated by the law. If Allie wished to, she could simply take a long vacation and let the company grind itself into the dirt. But that would, at least in my opinion, not be acting honorably. That very certainly would not be her father's wish. I think we can agree on that."

In the end, after reviewing the list of companies under the Kalkan umbrella, Allie authorized Rufus Sapp to begin proceedings to have her father declared incompetent.

"I don't know how to run the company," said Allie. "We have people in the office, there are managers in all the outer offices. But I don't know what to do."

Sapp closed the file folder and ran his hand over it as if to smooth out any wrinkles.

"A thought for you to consider," he said. "Although your father and Malcolm Crawley had their ups and downs, your father always trusted him explicitly. And Crawley knows the company. He had a hand in building much of it. Why don't you think about bringing him on in a temporary capacity to help you with these decisions that are going to be demanded of you?"

Allie had never given Crawley much thought. Although having spent years working in the same building, their worlds seldom intersected. Crawley's sole focus was on her father. He was polite to the old man's daughter, but never overly gracious. Allie may well have been the only female biped under the age of fifty Crawley had not propositioned.

"I think that's probably a pretty good idea, Rufus. I truly don't know what I think should happen to the company. I'm sure Malcolm will be able to offer some guidance."

Roberta's mouth opened but she did not speak. From her desk just outside Khalil's door she had been witness to Crawley's ambitions of personal wealth at the expense of the company too many times to mention. This was, she knew, a terrible idea. She also knew that it was never going to be her place to talk Allie out of it. She genuinely cared for Allie and was sorrowed by what the woman was going through. But Roberta knew that she was a hired hand and nothing more.

"Could I ask you to reach out to Malcolm for me?" Allie asked Sapp.

"I'll do it today," he replied. "Look for Malcolm to be in touch immediately."

As the women drove back to the Kalkan headquarters, Rufus Sapp called his old friend.

"It went just as I thought it might," said the attorney into his phone. "Give it a day and then call her. She's swimming and is in desperate need of a life preserver."

Crawley sat at the desk in his den. It was good to be back in the game. It was a lucrative position his friend Rufus Sapp had put him in. They had done deals together before, but none ever approached the size and scope of selling off a company worth a quarter of a billion dollars. This was going to be a huge payday for both of them.

Allie met Malcolm Crawley at the main entrance and escorted him to the elevator and back up to the third floor. Their telephone conversation from two days earlier was brief. Yes, he would be willing to help operate the company. Yes, his old office would be fine. The notion of selling assets never came up. It was Crawley's intention to let things get a little hairy, to let a few contrived-or-not bombs go off, to lay the groundwork for this suggestion. He had discussed this strategy with Rufus Sapp. Real money, big dollars can change hands when big ticket items are bought and sold. And the seller is quite often not the only party to realize the proceeds. People involved with or even simply on the perimeter of big deals can find a way of skimming profits from the larger pool. Crawley and Sapp knew this intimately. They both had been down the road traveled by Khalil Khan before.

"Who's on the fourth floor?" he asked as Allie showed him into his old office.

"No one. Well, Roberta's still up there."

"What the hell does she do all day?"

"I don't know, really. Daddy's phone still rings. She takes those calls and directs them to the appropriate people. I guess that's about it."

"I'm going to move her down here. We can have the phone re-directed. Anybody take Isabel's old office?"

"No," said Allie.

"Let's do that, then. I'll talk to her. In the meantime,

Allie, can you get someone in finance to bring me P and L's for the last six months for all divisions?"

"I'll be glad to, Malcolm."

Seeing Crawley exit the elevator on the fourth floor instantly gave Roberta Bertolli the creeps. He was dressed in black slacks and a burnt orange dress shirt, the sleeves of which were approximately one inch too short. His thin wrists were bony and untanned.

"Well, welcome back, Malcolm," she said. "What brings you back to Kalkan?"

She knew very well why he was back but was interested in whatever spin he was going to put on it.

"Hello, Roberta. I've been asked back on a temporary basis to help Allie run the company. I'll be here for a few months, at a minimum."

"Gosh, what a surprise," she said. "I had no idea. Please let me know if there's anything I can do to help, Malcolm."

"You can start helping by moving down into Isabel's old office. There's really no need to have anyone up here until we figure out what we're going to do with the company. I'll have Khan's line re-directed, so there won't be any missed calls. When they come in, I want you to direct them to me."

"OK, Malcolm. I'll start packing up my stuff and move down there this afternoon if that's alright."

"That will be fine, Roberta. I think we'll restructure your position here so that now you'll be working directly for me. You'll be my personal assistant. That might mean running some errands. Probably not a hell of a lot different from when Khan was here."

Roberta did not like the thought of working for Crawley,

but at least it was a job. It would do until she decided if she wanted to stay with the company or move on. She also did not like the way Crawley referred to her old boss by his last name. Khalil Khan had built an empire; he had created livelihoods for hundreds of people; he had provided the means by which many of his employees, not the least of which, Malcolm Crawley, had become well positioned financially. He deserved better than this dismissive reference, at least in her mind.

"Just let me know what you need me to do, Malcolm," she said.

"Let's start by having you call me Mr. Crawley," he said as he turned and headed back to the elevator.

The list of errands was nothing she hadn't done for Mr. Khan, but they rankled her. Where Mr. Khan had always been polite in asking her to get him lunch at the diner or to pick up his laundry, Crawley directed her to do so with not an ounce of gentility. He never offered to buy her lunch. And he never thanked her.

It was a week after Crawley's return that she decided to begin looking for another job. Her position as Crawley's assistant was not fulfilling. She also wanted to burn her clothes after spending any amount of time at all in his office.

"Maybe it's because you were always behind that desk outside of Khan's office, Roberta, but I never really noticed how attractive you are. You have a very nice body."

"Thank you, I guess," she said. She was sitting across from his desk taking notes on one of the dozen legal pads she found when she moved into her old lover's office. She derived a subtle and indefinable pleasure out of using Isabel's old stuff.

"We should maybe get a drink one night after work," he said. "What do you think?"

"I think that might cross a line I'm not willing to cross, Mr. Crawley. I don't know as how that would be appropriate. I don't think Mr. Khan would approve if he were here."

"Fuck Khan," he said derisively. "You work for me now. You don't want to get a drink, you don't want to be my friend, that's fine. But don't ever throw Khan in my face again, Roberta."

"I'm truly sorry, Mr. Crawley. That was not my intention."

"We're done here," he said waving her out of his office.

She walked down the hall and into the office she now shared with Isabel's ghost. She wanted to cry but did not. She wanted to feel, just once more perhaps, Isabel's moistened lips on her neck. She wanted to feel connected, as if somehow, miraculously, she was not alone drifting on a tide in the middle of the ocean.

Rufus Sapp visited Kalkan two weeks into Crawley's ascension. He sat with Crawley and Allie in the third floor conference room. Roberta had joined them at Crawley's invitation. She sat silently with crossed legs. Isabel's pad of paper and pen rested on the table in front of her.

"I don't think I've ever been in this conference room," said Sapp. "Whenever I met Khalil, it was always on the top floor. How is your daddy doing, Miss Allie?"

"He seems to be comfortable. The place we found for him is remarkable. They take such good care of him. He'll never recover his senses…that's what they tell me. I guess he had a minor stroke in addition to everything else. But at least he's comfortable. I see him on Sundays, right after I teach bible school."

"You want a coffee or something, Rufus? Roberta, why don't you get Mr. Sapp a cup of coffee?"

Sapp raised his hand.

"Thank you, Roberta. But no thank you."

Sapp had come bearing gifts for Malcolm Crawley. He delivered the court order declaring Khalil Khan incapacitated to Allie. He also had prepared a document naming Crawley as the acting co-director of the company. He would share responsibility for the company with Allie; his directives would carry equal weight. Sapp had discussed this with Allie two days earlier, and had convinced her that a more seasoned hand, someone with Malcolm's knowledge of business and familiarity of the company's workings would be of critical importance. She could always go to court in the event Malcolm's actions were too far from what she thought they should be. But at least on a temporary basis, Sapp easily convinced her, elevating Crawley to this position was in everyone's best interest.

When the meeting had ended, Crawley directed Roberta to escort Rufus Sapp out of the building.

"Let's chat," he said to Allie.

"Pull the door shut, Roberta. See you, Rufus."

Crawley poured himself a glass of water from the pitcher and matching set of three tumblers his personal assistant had placed on the table.

"Water?" he asked Allie.

She shook her head.

"I guess we're kind of partners now, aren't we?" she said.

"I think all of us are just sick at what happened to your father, Allie. And then add to that what Buster did. I don't know how you're holding up."

"I have my faith," she said. "I have my work with young people."

"Listen" he said, "I want to run a concept by you. Just so you can let it settle in. Let it percolate a little."

"OK, Malcolm. What?"

"Your father owned…your father *owns* the entire company. All the assets. Everything. He'll never be able to run it again, and that's a shame. But I want you to ask yourself if running it is something you want to do. I mean, you've seen what kind of energy and commitment it takes just to keep the walls from closing in…at least you've seen a piece of this since I left, and Isabel quit. I want you to ask yourself if you want to do it."

There was a quick rap on the door and Roberta poked her head in.

"You're not needed right now," said Crawley. "This is personal."

Roberta looked at Allie and wondered if it was simply her imagination that Khalil Khan's daughter looked as might a lamb being led to slaughter, that the lack of eye contact indicated she knew of her own imminent fate?

"The door please," said Crawley.

After a moment of digestion, Allie nodded her head and looked at Crawley.

"What do you think we should do, Malcolm. I know you've said that your return to Kalkan isn't going to be permanent. And I really don't know if I want to run this big company. I don't know…and this is me being one hundred percent honest with you, Malcolm…if I know how to run Kalkan. It's so huge."

"If we sell Kalkan, either as one entity, or in parts to regional buyers around the country, you'll have more money than you'll know what to do with, Allie. Your father will be taken care of for as long as he lives. Think about it. Think of the good you could do with money like that. Think of the people you could help. Maybe your church."

Allie was silent.

"Just give it some thought, Allie," said Crawley.

"I have. I have already. I know that daddy would hate the thought of selling what he worked for all those years. But I don't know if I have another option. I mean, we could hire another Vice President. Find another Isabel. But who would she report to? Who would be there for her?"

"This is my point," said Crawley. He poured another glass of water.

"OK," she said. "Let's do it. Let's sell Kalkan."

Crawley sipped at his water.

"I don't have a clue as to how we should go about this," Allie said.

"Leave everything to me, Allie. Your father trusted me and so can you. I'll take care of everything."

Crawley had laid the groundwork. Years earlier, when Khalil Khan had entertained the notion of taking his company public, Crawley was tasked with finding the right investment firm to do so. After countless meetings and tiring trips to all of the outer markets to perform due diligence, the firm sat ready to sell a couple hundred million dollars' worth of Kalkan stock. The deal fell through when Khan, in a knee jerk reaction to God-knows-what, had stated that the agreed upon amount wasn't enough."

"Listen" he told the investment guys who were seated in the fourth floor conference room with the old man and Crawley, "for what I'm talking about doing with my company, for where I'm thinking of taking this company, a couple hundred million is not enough. I'm thinking on global terms. I'm talking about a billion dollars. So, sell some stock or sell some debt, but that's my number."

The head of the investment company's team of three closed the notebook in front of him. It was dark blue and was embossed with the firm's logo. It contained preliminary agreements that, when signed by Khalil Khan, would start the ball rolling toward the influx of many millions of dollars. But this was not happening. People tasked with handling huge sums of money are rarely able to look the other way when crazy comes out of the box.

"Walk me to my car," he said to Malcolm Crawley.

"We'll be in touch," he said to Khan.

The deal had crashed, but Crawley had maintained a working relationship with John Sullivan, the point man for the investment firm who had walked out of Khan's conference room. Sullivan had climbed his own ladder and was now head of international investment. That meant that he found properties for wealthy Asian investors. Other nationalities were represented; Sullivan flew several hundred thousand miles a year all over the world. But the real money, the limitless wells of wealth, were in China, Korea and Japan.

"I'm very sorry to hear about what happened to your boss," he told Crawley from his fortieth-floor office in Manhattan. "There certainly were signs of something like this developing, even all those years ago, weren't there?"

"Yea. It happened really fast at the end there," said Crawley. "Kal's son killed himself. That sort of put the old man over the edge, you know?"

"Tragic," said Sullivan. "Anyway, I've got a team of three heading your way next week. My assistant, Michael, will reach out to you and let you know details. I suspect you know the drill, Malcolm. Due diligence trips, valuation assessments, lots of late nights with your financials."

"Yes. I'll be the point person for the company. Khan's daughter, I don't believe you met her when you were here before, she's the co-pilot with me on this. But to be completely honest, John, she's not the brightest bulb on the tree. Most of this will be significantly over her head."

"Understood," said Sullivan.

At the end of the day the company fetched a touch under three hundred million. The odd businesses here and there, the ones that didn't seem to fit, the diners, the car lots, the golf course in Virginia, the health spas, were sold off to anyone willing to buy them. The meat and potatoes of Kalkan, the television stations, the telecommunications group, anything even slightly touching the NFL, all went to an investment consortium out of Shanghai. The young Chinese man and woman who visited Kalkan headquarters both wore very high-quality, navy blue suits. Their shoes were Italian. They had both been educated at Duke, and their English was spot on.

Although an enormous sum, more than would last several lifetimes, Allie was surprised by how little of the sale price reached her. Rufus Sapp had put her in touch with Melinda Beatty, a personal investment banker, and Beatty had developed a multi-company portfolio for Khan's daughter.

"I know that's a crazy amount of money," said Allie.

She was sitting in Beatty's office reviewing the portfolio that had been prepared for her. As she often admitted to swimming in numbers concerning the business, Allie now swam in stocks, bonds and tax shelters, gold, silver and platinum.

"I know that it's crazy, but an awful lot of money went to the investment company and to the lawyers. So many people had to be involved in this. I don't even know who all of them were."

"A hundred million dollars is a lot of money, Allie. Regarding the deal, I don't know all those details. But I will tell you this: in order to make money, you have to spend money. And you still have your father's personal real estate to sell. And your brother's."

Allie had no way of knowing that Melinda Beatty was a life-long friend of Rufus Sapp. Although every penny Sapp earned as part of the transaction team was legal, his slice of the pie was several thousand percent higher than normal. As was Malcolm Crawley's.

When Allie had approved the package created by her new investment agent, when she had left the building and headed home, Melinda Beatty called her old friend.

"She's happy. We fixed her up in some very sound markets. She'll have no worries," she told Sapp.

"You're a dear, Melinda."

Allie immersed herself in the workings of her church. She visited her father twice a week and read him spy novels. He had often professed an interest in them, but never, at least that she could recall, took any time away from running the empire he had built to pick one up.

She saw the boy from the basement at church but brought him home with her less and less often. He was in college now and was home only on the occasional weekend. He was often accompanied to Sunday services by a pretty girl in a sundress. Her hair was the color of wheat, and her face was covered with freckles.

Not often, but regularly, Allie met Roberta for lunch at what used to be her father's diner. The food had not improved but the women felt like it was the right place to meet.

Roberta left Kalkan as soon as she secured a new job. The head of operations for a home security company needed a personal assistant who could double as an accounting clerk, and Roberta fit the bill. Her new boss was neither educated nor sophisticated. He had worked his way up the chain of command. He had started as an installer of home security systems and learned the business from the ground up. He didn't wear a suit. His car was not new and was not foreign. He worked incredibly hard, and he treated Roberta with courtesy.

Relative to the kookiness she had lived for many years at Kalkan, her new job was dull. But it was a paycheck, and it was steady. It bothered her less than she would have expected that she seemed to have almost overnight turned into her parents. What bothered her more and more was that she was alone.

Norman knocked on the door of Ella's classroom before entering. She had caught up to him in the hall earlier in the day and asked him to stop by after the kids had left for the day.

"C'mon in, Norman. Welcome back to school."

"Welcome back, yourself," he said.

"Please come in and join me for a while."

He squeezed into one of the small chairs. Ella sat on the edge of her desk, her long legs dangling over the side.

"I think I know what this is going to be about," he said. "It's about Martha, isn't it?"

"I have to ask," said Ella, "I mean, it's obvious that she's going to have a child. I just want to know if you, or if she needs any help. I don't need to know your business. I'm just reaching out as a member of our tribe. We should support our own people, and that's what I want to do."

"We don't know if it's mine. She was with one other man before me. It's not like she's a slut…"

"I would never say that," Ella interrupted. "A woman's body is her own and no one should be allowed to pass judgement on things like that."

Norman nodded.

"How is it living with your brother?" asked Ella.

"It's good. I think we keep each other out of trouble. I never really got into any trouble, so his part is easy. He's been in trouble a lot."

"This is my point, Norman. The world does not care about Natives. We need to be there for each other at all costs. If someone had been there for Peter, maybe his life would have been different."

Norman sat in his green work clothes on his tiny chair and let this sink in.

"We think the baby's mine," he said unable to contain a wide smile. "We're pretty sure."

"Are you excited?"

"There's a problem," said Norman.

"Let me help," said Ella. Her eyes did not look away from his face.

"She took some money from this church. She was going to have the baby and give it up for adoption, and the church offered her thirty thousand dollars...half now and half when the baby was born. She took half of the money."

"Have her give it back. For fuck's sake, it's a church. They're not going to do anything."

"Her brother took it. He was staying with her, and he talked her into loaning it to him to buy a car and get moved to a job in Ohio someplace. Anyway, he's gone and so is the money."

What church?"

"The Son of God church. That place on Water Street."

"That's my fucking neighbor," said Ella. "That's the asshole who lives next to us...next to me. The racist. That's his church."

"I don't know," said Norman. "But we, Martha and me, we need to figure something out. We want to keep this baby, but who has fifteen thousand dollars laying around? She signed a contract."

Ella thought for a moment. She stood from the edge of her desk. Not a physically demonstrative woman, especially with men, she stood next to Norman and placed a hand on his shoulder. It was the first physical contact of any type between the two. He sat rigid.

"I want you to talk to Martha and ask her if it's OK that I talk to Raif Hostettler. I don't really have any kind of relationship with him. We used to wave to each other once in a while. But I might be able to find a way out of this. I mean, they're not going to take someone's baby against her wishes. Just see if Martha wouldn't mind if I spoke to him."

Ella knew good and well that she was going to talk to her neighbor. Seeking Martha's permission was a formality.

Ella Crow was destined to never have children of her own. She knew this and was comfortable with it. In no small part, it was why she had chosen the career path she had. Although Norman was older than she was, she recognized the fact that he was incapable of dealing with this problem face on. Norman was a slinker, a man who had grown up intentionally in shadow. This was her job, as a member of a people who never seemed to get a fair shake, to right a potential wrong.

She talked about it that night with Isabel. They sat on beach chairs in the yard separating Ella's house from her hay pasture. Autumn at this latitude comes early, and the evenings had begun to cool. They wore hooded sweatshirts and sipped red wine out of coffee cups.

"I can tell you that this church would not have a right to that child in a million years," said Isabel. "To fall back on a contract that was one inch away from buying and selling a human being would be idiotic."

"That's what I thought, too," said Ella. "I don't know. I'm going to go and talk to him. Maybe this weekend."

"You want me to go with you?" asked Isabel.

"You gonna protect me, Izzy?"

The women sat and enjoyed the sun going down. Isabel talked a bit about her career as a businesswoman, in dealing with the jerks like Malcolm Crawley, of taking men in the boardroom by surprise with her preparedness and confidence.

"You miss it?"

"I miss the rush. I miss the excitement."

"Maybe you could start a business here, Iz."

"Yea. One more fudge shop to make the tourists even fatter than they already are."

Ella walked up the long dusty drive to the Hostettler farmhouse. She knocked on the brown door to the side of the house and was greeted by a diminutive and mousy woman wearing an ankle-length dress and blouse buttoned to her throat.

"Can I help you?" asked the woman.

"Hi, I'm Ella Crow, your neighbor. I live in the next farmhouse over, the one with the blue shutters. I was wondering if your husband, if Raif was around."

"He is. I'll get him."

Ella stood three steps down and waited. She took inventory. No animals. No equipment. Clearly not a working farm in any way.

Raif opened the door and smiled down to her. He wore jeans and a tee shirt with no shoes or socks. There was dirt under his toenails. An elaborate neckless of a crucifix made of two nails hung outside his slightly graying shirt. He was not a small man, but Ella could see as she took him in from the bottom step that she was a good two inches taller.

"Come on in, neighbor," he said holding the door for Ella.

"Why did you make her stay out there and wait?" he said to his wife who stood in an archway separating the kitchen from an interior room.

"Why didn't you invite her in?"

"Sorry," said the woman as she looked down and folded her fingers together.

Ella stood in the kitchen and took inventory. Neat as a pin.

"Sit," said Hostettler to Ella as he motioned to straight-backed chairs and a kitchen table that were clearly two decades old.

Ella sat and placed her hands as if in prayer on the table.

"We've never been what you might call close neighbors," she said, "other than the occasional salute on the highway kind of thing, but there's a matter I need to talk to you about."

Raif took a seat across the table from Ella.

"Shoot."

"It's about the Native man who used to rent the apartment above my garage, Norman Tall Tree. It's about him and his girlfriend. Her name is Martha Lapeer. I think it has something to do with the church you go to."

Hostettler ran his hand through his hair. He was Ella's age, but looked older, as if had lived the first half of his thirties twice. He smiled crookedly with teeth the color of caramel. Although he had not shaved in days, Ella noticed the tracings of acne scars on his face. He stood and walked to a counter. He took a cigarette out of a pack and lit it with a kitchen match. Ella smelled the smoke and sulfur in equal parts.

"I know who she is. I don't know him, but our church made arrangements for her baby to be adopted. We found a nice couple downstate. Good, clean, Christian people who will provide for that baby, who will raise that baby right."

Ella nodded. Hostettler exhaled blue smoke in the direction she was sitting.

"They don't want the baby to be adopted. Martha and Norman, he's the baby's father, they want to raise the child. They don't want the deal to go through."

"Not a problem," said Hostettler. "Just tell her to return the money the church gave her. It was to cover the doctor and hospital bills. It was fifteen thousand. She got fifteen thousand and was to get another fifteen thousand when the baby was delivered to the family. Tell her to return that money and the deal's off. That wasn't the church's money. That money came from the family."

"She doesn't have it, Raif," said Ella. "Long story, but her brother got a hold of it. That money's gone."

"Well, I guess she's up a creek without a paddle," he said.

Ella tapped her hands on the table as if preparing for a drum solo.

"Listen, I spoke with an attorney. One of the legal aid guys at the tribe. He says there no way in hell this little contract of yours is binding on anyone. It's close to buying a human being, for god sakes."

"This isn't the first one of these we've encountered. We've had girls before who wanted to back out. And you're right, there's not a hell of a lot we can do about it. If they don't want to pay the money back, they don't have to pay the money back. Our beautiful court system always rules on their side. So, we see what they own. I believe your little friend there has a house. We'll slap a lien on that. Maybe the church can get its money back over the long run, when she dies, and the house is sold."

"That house is all that woman has," said Ella, her voice slightly raised. "I'm sure she would want to keep it in her family."

"Maybe you go get your tribe to pay off her debt," said Hostettler. "Maybe you get someone other than a white man to pay off the debt she owes. You know, I'm sick of you people squeezing out babies without considering how the fuck you're going to take care of them. You're like, fuck it, let the white man take care of it. That's your mindset."

Ella stood and went to the door.

"I'm glad I stopped here," she said. "I had a hunch you were a racist asshole. Now I know."

"Have a great day," said Hostettler.

"How'd your meeting with your neighbor go?" asked Isabell.

"As expected, I suppose. We were right. There's nothing they can do to take that baby, but he brought up some crap about placing a lien on poor Martha's little house. She'll never have fifteen grand or anything close to that."

"At least that should give them some piece of mind that no one's going to take their child."

Ella and Isabel were eating lunch at one of the small tables in the cafeteria. Children sat at every table and the high-pitched noise that filled the room resembled cicadas in season.

"Yea," said Ella. "I hate white fuckers like that. He suggested that I get the tribe to pay them off. Like my people haven't had to suffer because of whites enough already."

Isabel took a forkful of salad.

"Ella, just because he's white, doesn't explain the fact that he's a pig. I mean, I'm white, right?"

"You know what I mean," said Ella. "I can't pretend that it's not there."

"That what's not there?" asked Isabel.

"Racism. Systemic racism against natives. I refuse to look the other way."

"And I haven't walked in your shoes," said Isabel.

"Thank you for not saying moccasins," said Ella. She reached across the table and brushed Isabel's hair away from her forehead. It was a rare display of affection, especially in front of the children. Isabel wanted to believe that it was Ella's way of acknowledging that the race issue need not always be the only issue. But she was pretty sure it was just a signal that the conversation was over.

The next morning Isabel dressed for the gym. She sat at her table in the kitchen and sipped a cup of coffee. She had begun to enjoy the off-days from her volunteer work. It wasn't as if she had loads to do; her house was always clean, and her laundry never piled up more than one load's worth.

She had connected quickly and rather intensely with Ella Crow. It had simply become apparent that a little Ella Crow could go a long way. One of the things she loved about Ella, her unyielding passion, could also become an annoyance. There was very little moderate temperature in Ella's universe; it was hot, or it was cold. Almost always.

She drove to the gym on campus. At eight in the morning the gym was rarely busy. Kids would be in classes or sleeping in. Isabel's routine was to pound away for an hour on a treadmill or elliptical machine, to stretch for thirty minutes, to do a little strength work with light dumbbells, and then stretch for a final ten minutes or so. This she did four or five days a week.

She was surprised to see a woman speed-walking on one of the treadmills. Usually, kids from the school were her only companions. The ramp was elevated, and the woman climbed in place with long and steady strides. Her arms were bent at each elbow and powered back and forth as pistons.

Isabel stepped on to an elliptical machine behind the woman and began her workout at a lower setting of difficulty. As the minutes and calories added up, she added degree of difficulty to the setting. At forty minutes, the other woman finished on her treadmill and walked to a water cooler in one of the corners of the gym. She noticed Isabel behind her and waved. Both women smiled.

Isabel powered down and joined the woman at the water cooler. The woman was older than Isabel but was in equally terrific shape. She had blonde hair that fell loosely to her shoulders. Her eyes were brilliantly blue and expressive. Even standing there in sweatpants and a sport top, sweating freely from her workout, Isabel had to notice how attractive the woman was.

"Quite a workout," said Isabel as she filled the paper cup from the water cooler.

"You know," said the woman, "I'm traveling, and just

don't get these in as often as I want to. This gym is a godsend. The hotel has a deal with them. It's a nice little perk."

"Business or pleasure traveling?" asked Isabel.

"Business," said the woman. "I come up here about four times a year. To see clients."

"May I ask what type of clients?"

"Sure," said the woman. "We do hospitality events. I arrange for different venues throughout the state. There's a ton of logistics, trust me. I come up and meet with the various hotels and restaurant people to keep the lines of communication open."

Isabel re-filled her paper cup.

"You?" asked the woman.

"Oh, I live here. I live here in town. I just use this gym. It's about the only top-notch amenity Sault Ste. Marie has to offer. Unless you fish."

"Do you work here? By the way, my name's Annie. Annie Merkel."

"Isabel Storey."

They shook sweaty hands.

"I don't work," said Isabel. These words carried substance. Her face stiffened from the smile it had been wearing. "I did work. I ran a company out of Memphis. You know, the grind. Several hundred employees, lots of pressure."

"What do you do now?"

"I'm figuring that out, actually. I'm enjoying a little down time. I volunteer at an elementary school. To be honest, I'm getting a little bored. I'm not sure I want to jump back in totally with both feet, but I can feel that I'm going to do something."

"Good luck to you, Isabel. It was nice chatting with you."

"Same to you, Annie."

Isabel tossed her used cup into a trash can. She resumed her position on the elliptical machine and began grinding away as she watched the woman walk out. Isabel's job had been exponentially bigger than this woman's, it had carried with it tons more responsibility, it had paid significantly more. But Isabel was not her job any longer. She was, in an odd way, less than this woman. Her mind raced with possibilities as drops of her sweat fell steadily on the moving track beneath the machine. She had details to work out.

Paul Sundeen was reading a Penthouse Magazine when Isabel walked into his office. He quickly placed the magazine on his desk and covered it with a file folder.

"I read the articles," he said sheepishly.

"No doubt," said Isabel. "Do you have a minute?"

"Of course. Please, sit."

"I have to break my lease. I have to relocate again, and I need to ask you about the few items of furniture in the house. I want them to go to a woman named Martha Lapeer, but I'm not sure when she'll be able to make arrangements to get them. It might take a week or so. Will that be a problem of any sort?"

"No, not at all. I'm sorry to see you leave. New job or something?"

"Something along those lines," she said.

Isabel took a checkbook out of her handbag and began filling in a check.

"I believe the lease said three months, right?"

"That's correct, but only make the check out for two.

Your security deposit will cover the third month. I'm sure that you've kept the place in good shape."

"Why, thank you, Paul. Could you write me out a receipt?"

He hunched over his receipt book as if keeping cheating eyes away from his test answers.

"Where are you going?" he said without looking up.

"Boston," she said.

"Work or pleasure," said Sundeen with a condescending smile.

"Hopefully, a little of both," said Isabel.

He tore the receipt out of the book and slid it across the desk.

"Good luck, Isabel. Hopefully, you'll come back and visit us one day."

She thought of Ella. She though of Norman and Martha.

"Perhaps," she said. "Oh, I'll be out of the house by Friday. If you could give Ms. Lapeer an extra week to get the stuff out of the house, that would be great. I'll have her drop the keys off after they're done."

"Always willing to accommodate someone as pretty as you, Isabel."

"You're too kind."

Isabel drove her car to Ella Crow's and parked in the driveway. Ella was not yet home from school, so Isabel sat on the steps leading into the kitchen. She would miss this view. She would miss the hikes around Hostettler's place up the hill to the rocks. She would miss Ella's bigness, her cooking, her laugh. She would miss the sex. Ella could be a pain in the ass with all the crusading, but she was a wonderfully-skilled lover.

When Ella's truck pulled in, she stood and walked out to greet her. Ella wore a quizzical look. Isabel leaned in through the open driver's side window and kissed her lightly on the lips.

"What a nice surprise," said Ella. "I thought you were staying home tonight."

"I've got some news," said Isabel.

"That's two of us," said Ella.

They opened a bottle of wine and sat in the yard.

"You first," said Isabel.

Ella sipped wine from her coffee mug.

"Remember when I told you that I talked to that lawyer from the legal aid office at the tribe?"

"Yea. He said the baby contract was bullshit, right?"

"Yea, but we also talked about law school. We talked about me going to law school. He told me that if I was interested, he was pretty sure he could get the tribe to pay for it. All of it."

"Oh my God," said Isabel. "That's fantastic."

"He called me today. He left a message at the school for me to swing by and see him. He worked it out, Iz. I'm going to law school starting next year. My next few years will be nine months in Lansing and then three months back here at the farm. Think of the good I will be able to do for my people. Think of the changes I can make."

Isabel placed her mug on the ground. She rose and stood behind Ella. She hugged her from behind.

"I'm so proud of you," she said. "You're going to make a fucking fantastic lawyer."

"Alright, sit," said Ella. "Tell me your news."

"It's not as exciting as yours, but it also involves a move. I'm going back to work. I don't really know what this little adventure living here has been for me. I was sort of running from something, but I'm not worried about that, anymore. And I've loved being with you. God, I have loved that. But I need to get back in the game. And I can't do that from here."

"I knew this was going to happen," said Ella. "I had a hunch all along that this was going to be a steppingstone for you. I'll miss you, Izzy. I'll really miss you. But I'm happy for you."

The women sat and enjoyed a moment of silence as they digested each other's announcements.

"When are you going?" asked Ella.

"A few days. I told Sundeen that I wanted to give the furniture and stuff in my house to Martha. Maybe they could use your truck next weekend."

"That's very thoughtful of you. I'm sure we can take care of that."

"And one more thing," said Isabel.

She took the folded check from her back pocket and handed it to Ella. It was written on the Genesis Engineering account and was made out to cash for sixteen thousand dollars.

"There's an extra grand so that she can get an attorney to write some sort of release from that crazy fucking church. She can keep the rest for the baby."

Now Ella rose and stood behind Isabel. She placed her hands on her shoulders.

"I don't know if I've ever seen a kindness like this. I'm overwhelmed, Izzy."

"It's not that big a deal," said Isabel. "I have some money and I'm able to help, that's all."

Ella's hands slid beneath Isabel's shirt and bra. Her fingertips lightly brushed Isabel's nipples.

"You want to stay for dinner one last night?"

"I don't know if I'll ever be able to say no to that."

Raif Hostettler locked the door to the church behind him. He had been at a meeting of the elders that was called to discuss the Martha Lapeer situation. An attorney from the tribe had attended the meeting and had delivered a check written on the firm's account for fifteen thousand dollars. Before handing the check over, the church's president, an old and shriveled man who drove a pickup truck adorned with a decal of the confederate flag, was required to sign the release. He did so without speaking. When the attorney had left, the group remained for a few minutes. Some discussion was had concerning the plight of the white man in America, but it was without much enthusiasm.

Hostettler agreed to check all the doors, turn off the lights and lock up. As he left the church, his truck was the only vehicle remaining in the lot.

"Hey, fucker, want to dance?"

Hostettler turned to find a very large, dark skinned man a few yards behind him. The man had a ponytail of long black hair. It was close to dark outside, but Hostettler could see that the man was smiling.

"I don't want any trouble," said Hostettler to the man. "I don't even know you."

"No, you don't know me. You know my brother's girlfriend. That's who you know."

Raif Hostettler was not a small man. He had, as a boy, been in a few scrapes. To look at him, one would assume that he could handle himself in a situation like this. This assumption, on this occasion, would not be accurate.

When Peter Tall Tree walked into the apartment he shared with his brother, he went immediately to the chest of drawers that contained most of his clothes. He removed the blood-stained shirt he had been wearing and replaced it with a fresh one.

Norman watched all of this from his seat on the sofa. He had a sickening feeling in his stomach. He had enjoyed being responsible for his little brother for the first time in their lives. He had liked it that he was keeping his brother out of the kind of trouble that seemed always to find him. And he knew now, sitting there silently watching his brother change, that this was over.

"I'm going to the police station," said Peter. "I just beat the shit out of that guy from the church. The one who wanted the money back from Martha. I'm going to turn myself in."

Norman looked at the floor and shook his head.

"What good did that do, Peter. How did that help anyone?"

"Maybe he won't do it again," said Peter.

After Peter Tall Tree had walked the few blocks to the police station, after he had turned himself in knowing full well that he would be going back to prison as a three time offender, after the ambulance had taken a badly-beaten Raif Hostettler to the hospital for emergency surgery to correct, among other things, a ruptured spleen, a lacerated liver and a potential brain injury, and after all the other dust settled, Norman moved in with the soon-to-be mother of his child. He fawned over the younger woman. He wouldn't let her lift a feather. He treated her as he had never been treated in his life.

Hostettler remained in the hospital for three days before being transferred to the University Medical complex in Ann Arbor. After several surgeries and many days of rehabilitating his damaged brain and body, and many weeks later, he was transported to his home beside Ella Crow's farm. He could walk with the aid of a cane, his balance having been permanently impacted by the head injury. He could speak, but his wife was truly the only person able to decipher the gibberish. He would never again visit his church; the outdoor rallies filled with racist hate speech and threats would be held on some other person's farm. His days of solving easy crossword puzzles were over.

Mary Hostettler was a devoted wife. She had married her husband because no one else had asked. She looked the other way when he flirted with other women at church; she had tolerated the outdoor gatherings of angry men proclaiming to be victims of a society they now believed to favor people of color; she had stepped into and remained in the shadow cast always in her direction by a husband who could not be kind to anyone.

He had never struck her; his abuse was more subtle and cunning. Although their bank account was in both names, she rarely had spending money. When shopping was necessary, Raif drove her into town and waited in the truck while she went slowly up and down the aisles. She drove only when her husband wanted something but lacked the enthusiasm to get it himself.

On the occasions when Raif felt like sex, and although he knew it hurt her, he preferred to take her anally. His justification was that he enjoyed the tighter feel.

And she remained devoted to him. He was an invalid. He was entirely dependent upon her kindness. He could not live without her assistance. And this was going to be forever.

She cleaned him. She fed him. She wiped the spittle from his chin and face. She helped him move from chair to chair. But on occasion, when the thoughts of his nastiness took hold of her, after she had helped him change from pajamas to jeans and a shirt, and after she had helped him shuffle to his seat at the table, she fed him a breakfast of cold cereal doused in milk she knew had turned sour. The tuna casserole she made for him every Friday night was prepared with canned cat food.

On a Sunday morning three months after Raif sustained the injuries from which he would never recover, Mary positioned her invalid husband comfortably in an easy chair in front of the television set. She turned to a station broadcasting a church service. He seemed to like this.

She walked quickly into the guest bedroom in which she had slept since her husband's return from the hospital. She carried a large suitcase she had packed the day before through the kitchen, down the steps across the gravel drive, and hoisted it up into the passenger side seat of Raif's truck.

She went back in the house to grab up her purse. In it were her set of house keys, a tube of lipstick and a certified check she had taken away from the bank earlier in the week when she had closed their joint account. She said nothing before closing the door behind her.

At Ella Crow's house, she climbed down from the truck and went to the door.

"Oh, hello," said Ella. "Raif's wife, right? Everything OK?"

"It's fine, thank you. I need to ask you to do something for me."

Ella had stepped down the stairs and was standing face to face with her neighbor.

"Sure," she said. "What's up?"

"I need you to call the police and tell them that you're worried about Raif maybe being home alone. Maybe you could say that you drove by and noticed his truck was gone. That you are concerned. But please don't call them until this afternoon. I want to get as far away as possible before they find him."

"I'm not sure I understand," said Ella. "Do you want to come in and have a cup of coffee or something?"

"No, thank you. I'm leaving. I'm leaving him. I'm going to go stay with my sister in Indiana. I won't take care of him any longer."

"I'm sorry for what happened to him," said Ella.

"About that," said Mary Hostettler, "I would like you to do one more thing for me if you would."

She reached into her purse and pulled out an envelope.

"It's five hundred dollars," she said. "Could you somehow get it to the Indian man who did this to my husband? I know he's in prison, and I know this money will be of help to him."

The world is filled with such hardships; bad things often happen to good people. We bear witness to these sorrows. We see hurtful people doing their worst to those we love. We experience pain and we wonder if the light outshines the dark. We wonder if there exists any true mechanism for administering justice. We question our authority to judge people and their deeds. And then we see Allie Khan. She is married.

The courtship was whirlwind, fueled along no doubt by the crumbling of Allie's world. But he is a good man. He works hard. He accompanies his wife when she visits her father at the nursing home.

They met through her work on the church board. At the gatherings following bible school, he was solicitous; he fetched her picnic cups of iced tea and cookies wrapped in a napkin. He was older but stepped lively.

Allie and Billy Tillman had much in common and were a good match. Neither of them drank. Despite having truckloads of money available to them, they preferred to stay home; travel held no interest. And on each Sunday night, after church services were over and after they had eaten their dinner and relaxed before Billy's workweek was to begin the following morning, they crept to the basement and reprised the reward and punishment bondage scene Allie had developed months ago with the young boy. At first, they took turns week to week. But in the end, they settled into the roles they preferred; Allie reveled in delivering discipline, and her new husband had a real taste for being punished.

And in a small town in northern Ontario in 1972 a girl was born to Cameron and Nellie Tootoo. The couple had settled on the shores of Lake Superior a year or so earlier. He had come to avoid the draft, and she had joined him a year later. Although they could have returned to the states, they loved their lives in Wawa. Nellie worked at a grocery store until, after many years, she was hired on as a teacher at the elementary school. Cameron relentlessly tried to find a place with the Ontario Provincial Park Service and was rewarded, after having jumped through the hoops necessary to reclaim his citizenship, with a job as a ranger in 1980. The couple bought a house on the edge of town. It was a sturdy, two-floor and unpretentious home that had been built thirty years earlier when the town was going through a bit of an economic uptick; the world starved for iron ore just then and the mine outside of Wawa enjoyed the sudden demand. In that home they looked after each other. They were both strong-spirited people, but voices were never raised. They were solid and loving parents to their daughter. Petra was a handful but was a respectful and beautiful girl. She had her mother's clumsy grace and her father's smile.

Roberta Bertolli was not eager to get home. She stayed at her desk until well past five. She was the last to leave.

The weekend had been a disaster. She had visited her parents and attempted to explain her sexual orientation to them. The Bertollis were nice people, but they had been forged in the fire of the Catholic Church; their list of sins was not negotiable. Cheating, lying, murder, suicide, even child abuse. Certainly, by their way of understanding God's rules, homosexuality.

"We will love you always," Roberta's mother had said, "but we can't accept this."

"I'm not sure where that even leaves us," said Roberta. "I gotta go."

Her drive home to her apartment in Memphis that Sunday night was empty. She was raw and was hurting. She felt alone as she had never felt before.

At work the next day she tried to keep busy, tried to push away the thought that she was, in a very real sense, without parents, was without their love and support. The effort failed. Finally, shortly after six, she packed up her things, locked the door to the office behind her and walked to her car.

"Hey, lady, you want to make out?"

She knew the voice and could not have prevented the tears had she tried. And she did not try. She dropped the big bag slung across her shoulder. It contained her life. Plastic lunch containers, keys, wallet, lipstick and a packet of tissues.

The embrace was full on. Both women were nourished by it. The entirety of the world around them vanished for those seconds. Nothing outside of their holding tightly to each other existed. Birds were silent as they watched the women below them.

"What are you doing back here?" said Arby. "How did you know where to find me?"

"It was easy. I went to Kalkan and asked around."

"What are you doing here?"

"Getting on with my life. I have to get a job. I have to create something, to produce something. I have to be with you, Arby. I need you in my life."

"I love you, Isabel," she said.

"Call me Izzy. It's a nickname I picked up along the way and I kind of like it."

Author's Note

This is a work of fiction. Although I have borrowed names common to geographical areas, all of the characters in this book are of my creation. Although this book takes place in parts of North America that are real, I have taken many liberties in describing these areas and in naming places within them.

I would like to thank Leni, Kate and Wendi for supporting this little writing habit of mine. They truly make me feel like a literary figure, or, as Doctor Sullivan would have said all those years ago: *a litrary figyah.*

Lastly, I want to thank the nuns teaching at St. Mary's School in Sault Ste. Marie, Michigan in the 1960's. They made certain that I was able to construct sentences and paragraphs with balance and grammatical soundness and they inspired me to read. Additionally, there can be very little doubt that their teaching methods left me, as well as many, many of my classmates, with a harmless yet deeply-felt fascination with corporal punishment. God bless them.

Printed in the United States
by Baker & Taylor Publisher Services